LITTERED WITH TROUBLE

A WHISKERS AND WORDS MYSTERY

ERYN SCOTT

KRISTOPHERSON PRESS

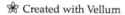

Welcome to Button, where everything's perfect except for the occasional murder.

Louisa Henry has had the *worst* year. She never imagined she would be a widow before the age of forty. To cope with the sudden loss of her husband, Lou moves across the country to live near her best friend in a town as cute as a button. Even though it means quitting her fancy New York editor job, she now owns the bookstore of her dreams.

Well, almost. She definitely didn't dream about a dead body showing up in her alley.

Found with no identification, the police plaster the man's face everywhere, along with the name of her bookshop, inundating Lou with negative press before she can even open. Worse, Lou was one of the last people to see him alive, and she didn't even get his name.

Worried the mystery man's family is left without the answers she so desperately needed in her husband's death, Lou tries to help find the man's identity. On closer inspection, she realizes her conversation with the mystery man was full of clues. Starting with a confusing book page he left behind, Lou follows the trail.

If she can solve this mystery, her bookstore might have a chance at being known for something more than murder.

Welcome to Button

1 - Button Books
2 - Material Girls
3 - Willow and Easton's houses
4 - George's Technology Emporium
5 - Bean and Button Coffehouse
6 - The Upholstered Button
7 - Button Bistro
8 - Pet Store
9 - Bakery
10 - Old Mansion

CHAPTER I

The bookstore sat on the corner of Thread Lane and Thimble Drive in the town of Button.

Tourists wandered the sewing-themed streets, bundled up in winter jackets to stave off the chilly January weather. Bags heavy with purchases hung from their arms as they scooted from one shop to the next.

Louisa Henry stood in front of the bookstore, a cat carrier at her feet.

Two large picture windows flanked the entrance and gave passersby a direct view inside, but the lights were off. The three-paned glass front door offered another glimpse of shadowy shelves and books lined up, cover to cover. The building's wood stained exterior had darkened with age, but the brightly painted trim around each large window kept it looking cheerful so it matched the adorable esthetic of the town nestled into the foggy Pacific Northwest.

Lou's gaze traveled up to the windows along the second floor that looked out from the apartment. Her new home. As much as she wanted to investigate that space, Louisa felt a pull

1

to start in the bookshop. She curled her fingers around the key in her hand until the metal bit into her palm. She needed the pinch of pain to remind her that this was all real.

After a deep breath that smelled of pine trees and woodsmoke, she stepped forward and used the key to unlock the front door of Button Books.

"Ready, Sapph?" Lou asked, glancing down at the cat carrier she'd set on the sidewalk.

She didn't expect a meow or even a blink of an almond-shaped eye in response. The white cat asleep in the carrier was deaf—as some white cats are—and had a habit of sleeping through exciting moments—as many cats do. Tapping on the side of the crate, she continued until he noticed the vibration. The cat peeled opened one jewel-toned blue eye, then two.

"Time to go in, buddy," she said.

Sapphire stretched and yawned, but immediately curled up again and went back to sleep. Lou chuckled as she picked up the crate. Her expectations about this moment piled up behind her and pushed her forward as she opened the door. A bell hanging around the handle jingled as the door closed behind her. She set down the cat crate and gave herself a moment to take it all in.

Lou could just barely discern the delightful, familiar smell of new bindings and freshly printed pages through the over-whelming scent of dust. The less-than-pleasant smell was to be expected. Willow warned Lou that the last owner had let the shop fall into disrepair. She'd been right. Button Books was a far cry from the adorable, cozy bookstore Lou remembered from her last visit to Button three years earlier.

Shelves that had been stocked full now contained more bare spaces than books. There were no longer any fancy pens or bookmarks for sale next to the register. Three of the five overhead lights didn't work when she flicked on the light switch. A layer of dust covered the love seat and two armchairs in the reading nook near the center of the shop. Haphazard stacks of books littered the table to her left, which she assumed was for customers to sit around. The floorboard she stood on creaked when she'd first stepped on it. A long cobweb wafted down from the corner of the ceiling.

Dozens of other differences announced themselves as Lou surveyed the rest of the space. It was at times like these that she was acutely aware that her unique attention to detail was both a blessing and a curse. Sure, it had made her a successful editor at a New York publishing house, but outside of work, it meant her mind often latched on to minutiae easily overlooked by others.

Despite the list of improvements she was still making in her mind, one feeling stood out among all the rest fighting for purchase inside Lou: adoration. She'd loved Button Books ever since the first time she'd visited the small Washington town a decade earlier, when her best friend had first moved here. The shop had been on her must-visit list during each subsequent trip. Purchasing it was one more step toward making a long-time dream come true.

She only wished her decision to buy the shop and move across the country hadn't come on the heels of so much loss. Ben's life insurance money had paid for the bookshop. The low ache of pain she carried with her at all times spiked at the thought of her late husband. She pictured Ben's smiling face. She could still hear his booming laugh and his baritone voice that carried across whole rooms—it had to when he taught Intro to English courses at NYU and lectured to classes full of freshmen.

As much as she and Ben had loved their life in New York

City, it had only ever been temporary. Their collective dream had been to work together, running an independent bookstore in a cozy small town.

"One day, it'll be just you and me, reading our lives away, LouLou," he'd said to her over and over throughout the years, so much so that it felt like a recording she could replay anytime in her mind.

"I did it, Ben," Lou whispered. "I just wish you were here." Her voice broke. She pressed her lips together.

Sapphire let out a loud meow as if he could sense she was thinking of his favorite person. Now that he was awake, Lou knelt next to the crate and opened the door, letting the cat inspect his new home. At first, he stepped along the worn wooden floors as if they were made of lava and might burn him. After a few minutes, the white cat strutted around the place like he'd lived there his whole life.

Goodness knew he was used to being surrounded by books. Living with an editor and an English professor had meant there was always a good stack of books around on which to fall asleep—and books had always been Sapphy's preferred napping location. True to form, he gracefully jumped up onto the crowded table to her left and curled up on the shortest stack of books.

"Looks like you approve," Lou said with a laugh.

Hanging her down jacket on the rack by the door, she pushed up the sleeves of her sweater and got to work.

She'd made a list of tasks and had dusted half the shelves by the time her best friend, Willow, showed up a few hours later. Willow blew inside like a winter gale had chased her down the street. Sapphire peeked open one eye at the rush of cold air.

"Hello!" Willow announced herself.

"Hi!" Lou called from where she knelt behind a bookshelf.

When Lou stepped out, a woman she'd known for thirty of her thirty-seven years on the planet was peeling herself out of a thick wool coat. Although Willow was tall and lithe like the tree she was named after, that was where the similarities ended. She didn't sway or drape or rustle softly through life. Willow, much like Ben, was loud and commanding—some might even say stubborn.

"I'd say you're settling in nicely, Sapphy," Willow said, greeting the cat with a delicate kiss on the head. Willow let her bag drop into an empty chair at the table and hung up her jacket next to Lou's. "Sorry I'm late. It takes so much longer than I expect to get ready for these sales."

Willow, a horticulture teacher at Button High School, held a plant sale each trimester to help raise money for upkeep on the school's greenhouse. Their late-January sale would take place tomorrow, and Lou was excited to grab some greenery to spruce up the shop. All the plants from her condo had stayed in New York. She'd been concerned they wouldn't survive the cross-country trek, so she'd scattered them among friends in the city as farewell gifts.

The two women's gazes finally met. Lou gave her friend a small smile. Willow lunged forward, wrapping her long arms around Lou. She squeezed tight—too tight, if you asked Lou— just as she always did.

"Honest three," Willow said into Lou's hair, repeating the phrase they'd used for decades to elicit a candid emotional check-in.

"Overwhelmed. Hopeful. Hungry," Lou responded, her words muffled by Willow's shoulder. Her friend invariably smelled like fresh air and soil, and Lou sank into the embrace.

Stepping back and releasing her, Willow said, "I can fix that last one." She returned to her large messenger bag and fished around for a moment before presenting a foil-wrapped burrito. She produced a second one after she'd handed the first to Lou. "It's either an early dinner or a late lunch, but I figured you would be too focused on the shop to think about food."

"Thank you. Have a seat." Lou grimaced as she gestured to the messy table in the front window.

Together, they moved most of the books to the floor nearby so they would have space to eat. They left Sapphire and his bookstack in place, knowing he'd had a long day of travel.

"Have you been upstairs yet?" Willow asked after she swallowed a bite.

Lou shook her head. Cassidy, the real estate agent, had taken her through a virtual tour of the two-bedroom apartment upstairs. It was lovely, but it wasn't what had pulled her here, and it could wait. Plus, Cassidy had met the movers here yesterday when Lou's flight had been delayed, and she'd reported that everything seemed in order. Cassidy had even convinced the movers to set up Lou's bed frame and mattress, so at least she would have a place to sleep tonight.

"I got distracted down here. I wanted to make some headway on my list before going upstairs." Lou took a bite of her burrito.

"Lou with a list." Willow clicked her tongue in a good-natured, teasing way. Her eyes widened. "Oh no. Speaking of lists. I'm just remembering there's one more thing on mine for tonight. I still have to print out the price stickers."

"Don't let me keep you," Lou said, waving a hand at her friend. "I should head up to the apartment soon, anyway."

"Okay, have a good first night." Willow stuffed her arms into the sleeves of her jacket and ducked under the strap of her messenger bag. "Call me if you need anything."

"I will." Lou waved as her friend took her half-eaten burrito and headed for the door.

"Oh ..." Willow stopped, one hand on the doorknob. "I forgot to say welcome to Button. I'm so glad you're here." She scrunched up her shoulders and grinned at Lou before leaving.

Lou returned the smile. She was glad she was here too. Even though she'd lived in New York for half her life, she'd spent the first half in Washington. She and Willow had grown up together just south of Seattle, and Lou had always felt like a Pacific Northwesterner at heart. Coming back to her home state felt right.

Her gaze traveled around the room again as she finished her burrito. The shop needed a lot of work, but she had time. While Ben's life insurance money had helped her purchase the building and the business, the sale of their Manhattan condo would be enough to give her the time and resources she needed to return Button Books to its former glory.

Shaking her head at that phrase, Lou said, "We won't just restore this place; we'll make it better. Won't we, Sapph?"

The cat twitched a whisker at her but didn't move besides that.

Once she threw away the foil wrapper from her burrito, Lou got back to work. The food had given her renewed energy. She was tucked behind another bookshelf, hard at work, when the front door opened again. The bell chimed. This time, instead of cracking open one eye at the change in temperature, Sapphy picked up his head. His blue eyes were wide as he stared at the door.

"Hello?" a man called. "Is there someone here?" His voice was tight.

Lou frowned. She warily pulled herself up off the floor.

"I'm here. What can I do for you?" Lou said softly, stepping out from behind the bookshelf.

The man locked eyes with her, rushing forward. He was tall, thin, and wore a beautiful navy suit under a long coat. His hair was a light brown and was slicked back, like he belonged in the nineteen twenties. A crease around the crown of his head told her he had been wearing a hat until recently. Small red marks on either side of his nose told the same story about a pair of glasses. His movements were erratic and his posture rigid. In one hand, he grasped at what appeared to be a single book page. His other fist was closed, but Lou couldn't see if he held anything in that palm.

"I must speak with the owner immediately. It's very important, urgent, really," he said without pausing once for breath.

"I'm the owner, but I'm afraid I'm not open yet. I just got the keys today, and it's going to take me a while to get the shop ready." Her gaze cut over to the door. She should've remembered to lock that when Willow left.

His hopeful expression fell. "You just bought it?"

"Yes." Lou studied the delicate mustache that covered the skin above his lip.

He dragged a hand through his hair but kept his thumb tucked into his palm as he did so. *Ah, so he was holding on to something in that hand.*

The man let out a shaky breath. "This isn't good. I must speak with the previous owner. Do you know where they are?"

Flinching at his intensity, Lou shook her head. "I'm so sorry. The last I heard, she'd moved away. Her name was Kimberly Collins, if that helps."

"Maybe it does. Maybe it doesn't. I don't know." He cleared his throat twice in a row before exhaling a wry laugh.

"Is Diana Moon Glampers running my life or what?" he added under his breath, slapping his palm onto his forehead.

Lou jerked back in surprise. Diana Moon Glampers? The Handicapper General from Kurt Vonnegut's short story, *Harrison Bergeron*? Ben had loved Vonnegut and included that short story in his syllabus each school year. Whenever things weren't going his way, he would jokingly wonder if Diana Moon Glampers had given him a mental or physical handicap.

"Hey there," Lou said, compassion for the man rising in her. "It's going to be okay. Would you like some tea?"

She'd noticed an electric kettle and some tea bags in the small kitchen in the back office earlier when she'd toured the space. Tea had always helped Ben calm down. Even though they looked nothing alike, there was something about him that reminded Lou of her late husband, and she wanted to help.

The man blinked at her. His shoulders settled an inch. "That would be lovely."

She motioned to the table, scooping Sapphire off the stack of books and tucking him under one arm. "Have a seat. I'll be right back."

The agitated man settled into the same chair Willow had occupied earlier. His right hand tapped out a staccato rhythm on the tabletop with a brass dimple key. She recognized the type of key as soon as she saw the smooth edges. Her old office had used the same kind, with the different sized cones cut in the blade instead of the standard teeth along the edge.

So that was what he'd been holding, Lou mused as she brought Sapphire with her into the office. The man might remind her of Ben, but she still didn't trust him enough to leave him alone with her cat. Settling Sapphy on top of the empty desk, Lou turned to face the wall that held a sink, cabinets, and a small refrigerator. She filled the electric kettle with water and clicked it on. Then she located a mug in the cabinet.

But just as she was fishing a tea bag from the box, the creak of a door opening was followed by the slam of one closing. Lou listened, frowning over at Sapphy.

"No bell," she said after a moment. *Weird ... unless he went out the back.*

She closed the office door behind her to keep Sapphire inside as she left to investigate.

The man was gone.

Outside the front windows, a winter sunset stained the sky a foreboding red.

CHAPTER 2

A͏fter the mystery man's sudden departure, Lou locked the back door, then did the same to the front. She checked the handle of the door that led upstairs to her apartment, satisfied that it was still locked tight.

"That was weird," she said with a shake of her head.

After one more sweep of the bookshop, she retrieved Sapphire from the office. The water was boiling in the kettle, so she turned it off and left it to cool. There would be no need for tea now that her visitor had left.

"I think it's time for us to go upstairs anyway," she told the cat, picking him up. "I'm obviously not thinking straight if I left a stranger in my bookshop unattended," she mused as she stroked the cat's fur. "That could've ended much worse."

He purred in response. Grabbing her purse and his travel crate, she unlocked the stairway door and headed up to the apartment. Boxes littered the space, but her bed sat assembled within the larger of the two bedrooms, just as Cassidy had promised.

The place was sweet. A stone fireplace in the corner of the

living room gave it a homey feel, and the kitchen was updated, though small. There was only one bathroom for the two small bedrooms, but what more did she really need?

Examining the boxes, she read the labels she'd put on each one, searching for any marked *Bedroom*. She needed to find her sheets if she was going to sleep. But the first box she opened held clothes. One of Ben's old sweatshirts sat on the top. Lou picked it up, holding it up to her nose. She breathed in the scent of him, though it was fading after so many months. Setting it aside, she opened another box.

After shuffling through a few boxes, Lou located her bedding. Sapphy's travel crate held water and food dishes, as well as a small litter box in the back, so he was taken care of for tonight. She topped off his food and slipped into bed, grabbing Ben's sweatshirt and pulling it close.

Sleep should've come easily after her long day, but her mind wouldn't turn off. She repeated the interaction with that man in her mind, hoping to notice something she'd missed the first time that might explain his sudden departure. She drifted off at some point, Ben's sweatshirt clutched tightly to her chest, and she woke the next morning with no further answers about the mystery man.

Lou had set an early alarm so she could get some work done before Willow's plant sale. Sapph was still fast asleep on the bed, so she left him upstairs as she padded down into the quiet bookstore.

Right away, her attention landed on the large garbage pile she'd accumulated during her cleaning yesterday. Preferring to start the day fresh, she began by stuffing the unwanted items into two garbage bags and hefting them toward the back of the store where the dumpster was located.

Lou unlocked the door and waddled into the alley, a bag in

each hand like a garbage-toting lady justice. But both bags fell to the concrete as they slipped from her grasp. Slumped against the back wall of her building was the man who'd visited her shop yesterday.

His skin was so pale, it was blue. His lips held almost no pigment. And, worst of all, his eyes were open, staring past her into nothingness. The cold January air wound around Lou's throat, making it impossible to scream. Despite the hundreds of questions running through her mind, one thing seemed certain: the man was dead.

Lou's gaze didn't leave the dead man as her fingers scrambled, searching her pockets for her phone. Shaking, she dialed the only person she could think of. The ringtone buzzed disapprovingly in her ear, reminding her that this was the second decision she'd made that would've had the New York version of herself shaking her head.

First, you leave a stranger alone in your shop, and then you call your friend instead of 9-1-1? her disappointed thoughts chided.

"Morning," Willow answered. A shuffling sound made Lou sure she was racing around with a million jobs to do for the plant sale that morning. "I'm just leaving. Did you need something?" A door closed in the background and keys jangled.

"The police." Lou's mouth was parched and cold, like she'd swallowed dry ice. "I need the police," she croaked the statement a little louder that time. "There's a dead man in my alley." The buildings seemed to spin around her.

To her credit, Willow didn't waste time gasping or asking questions. In fact, she didn't say anything to Lou at first.

"Easton!" she called, then started jogging if the crunching sound that followed was evidence. "Hey, I'm getting in."

A man let out a string of bewildered questions in the background. Lou wasn't confused, though. Willow's neighbor,

Easton, was a local detective. She must've caught him getting into his car just as she'd been coming out of the house.

"Yeah, you're driving me to Button Books. There's a body in the alley," Willow said. Car doors slammed. An engine revved to life before Willow spoke to Lou again. "We're on our way. I'm going to stay on with you. Can you talk?"

Lou swallowed. "Maybe." The word was as broken as Lou's heart felt.

"Don't talk, then. Just listen to my voice. We're only a couple of minutes out. Think about happy things: opening a brand new set of pens, the crack of a book spine the first time you open it, how satisfying it seems when Sapphy does one of those deep cat stretches." Willow paused for a moment, then added, "Think about Ben's laugh, Lou."

The statement was quieter than the others, and normally, Lou would've appreciated it. When Ben had first passed, Lou had confided in Willow that she didn't want to stop talking about him, or for people to be afraid to bring him up. The truth was, thinking about Ben was one of the things that made her the happiest—even if it ironically happened to be the thing that also made her the saddest.

Willow had been right to remind her of his infectious laugh. The thought usually brought an instant smile to her face. The problem was, she had already been thinking of Ben.

"The man is sitting up, slumped against the back of the bookshop. It looks like he's resting." Lou wrapped her free arm around her waist. She should've grabbed a jacket.

"Oh, honey. I'm so sorry." Willow's tone softened even more. She knew.

Lou had found Ben sitting in the same way.

The similarity made questions run through Lou's mind. Had this man died of a heart attack too? He didn't appear to be injured. The cold air wrapped around Lou's bare arms, reminding her he might've frozen to death. But if he'd needed a place to stay for the night, why had he run?

Details about the scene grabbed at Lou's mind. Ink stained the side of his right ring finger. The bottom of his shoes held scuffed remains of the de-icing chemical the city must sprinkle along the streets during the winter. Only one flap of his collar was buttoned, the other curled up a few centimeters, differing from his more polished appearance yesterday when she'd seen him.

"We're pulling up." Willow's voice broke through Lou's observations, causing her to flinch.

Hanging up the call, Lou tucked her phone in her pocket and listened as car doors slammed and footsteps echoed through the alley. Willow rounded the corner, Easton on her heels.

Willow spared a quick glance over at the body and winced. She wrapped an arm around Lou and angled her away. Behind them, the detective called for backup.

"You're freezing," Willow said, stepping over the garbage bags Lou had dropped. "I'm taking her inside to warm up," she called to Easton, who was kneeling next to the body.

"I need to get her statement." Easton frowned and stood.

"You can do that inside. I'm not keeping her out here any longer." Willow didn't wait for his response before she pulled open the back door and led Lou inside.

The mildly contentious interaction she'd just witnessed didn't surprise Lou. She'd heard all about Easton over the years. Willow complained about her grouchy neighbor constantly. The two of them butted heads like mountain goats. It had only gotten worse since Willow's fiancé, James, had left. Willow had always had a short fuse, but it had become almost nonexistent since James announced he was leaving her for one of his employees at the local bank. The only things that calmed Willow down were being in a garden and spending time with her horse—a horse Easton constantly complained about, hence the root of their unceasing strife.

Willow walked Lou over to one of the dusty chairs in the reading area, then disappeared into the office after saying something about tea. The room spun around Lou as she remembered doing the same thing for the mystery man when he'd stopped by yesterday.

Now he was dead.

Returning with a steaming mug, Willow placed the drink on the coffee table in front of Lou, who wrapped her fingers around it. She didn't think she could stomach drinking anything but holding the warm mug was a comfort.

"I just need to make a few calls for the plant sale." Willow held up a finger and walked to the other side of the room.

Disappointment surged through Lou. She didn't want Willow to miss her plant sale. Lou immediately quashed that feeling. This was a dead body. It was a big deal. Plus, Willow would be honest with her if she really needed to leave.

Minutes later, Willow settled in the chair across from Lou. "Okay, we're good." She stared at Lou for a moment before glancing toward the back door. "He couldn't have been home-less in a suit like that, but I didn't recognize him." Willow shivered.

"I did," Lou whispered.

Willow's eyebrows hitched higher on her forehead.

"He came into the shop yesterday. He was frantic." Lou explained the details she remembered about the encounter.

"Kimberly." Willow pinched the bridge of her nose after Lou had explained the part about him asking for the former

16

owner. "If I didn't know better, I'd say trouble follows that woman. But it's more accurate to say she invites trouble over with balloons and party favors."

As Lou recounted the events of her surprise visit yesterday, more vehicles had appeared in front of the bookshop. Two uniformed officers had spilled out of a patrol car. A man with silver hair, wearing a long wool coat, got out of a shiny black car. An ambulance had driven around the corner instead of stopping, so Lou figured that one had pulled around back.

Locals gathered on the sidewalk, heads bowed together.

The back door opened, and Easton strode toward them. He was rather tall, so Lou felt dizzy as she peered up at him from her seated position. His cheeks and nose were pink from the cold. He pulled off the heavy trench coat he wore, draping it on the love seat next to him as he sat. He wore slacks and a button-up, the gray tones in each piece of clothing complementing his tan complexion.

"I'm Detective West." He held a hand toward Louisa. "We haven't officially met."

"Lou." She took his icy hand and shook it. "I feel like I already know you," she added.

Easton's gaze flicked over to where Willow sat with her arms crossed. "Don't believe everything this one tells you." He jabbed a pen in Willow's direction, then clicked it open. "Can you walk me through how you discovered the body."

Lou swallowed, exhaled, and then started her story. Easton nodded as she mentioned the garbage, having noticed the bags sitting in the alley. His eyebrows rose, impressed, as she listed every detail she could remember.

"You noticed a lot." He flipped the notepad closed.

Willow snorted. "Not much gets past Lou," she said, almost as if it were a threat.

Easton ignored her, focusing on Lou. "Your mention of Kimberly Collins worries me. It sounds like she might be into something bad here, and I'd hate for you to get dragged into it. If I were you, I'd purchase a security system with cameras."

Lou fidgeted with the string on her tea bag. "Cameras? Why would I need—?" But she didn't finish her question.

Nausea swayed inside her, and she gripped her fingers tighter around the mug. She'd assumed the poor man had died of natural causes, like Ben. But Detective West's suggestion brought a terrifying possibility to light.

"The man out there was murdered?" Willow asked, giving a blunt voice to Lou's thoughts.

Easton nodded curtly. "As of right now, we're treating this as a homicide."

CHAPTER 3

The bookstore seemed to tilt unsteadily around Lou as she absorbed what Detective West had disclosed.

Murder.

The word crawled along her skin, making it itch. Disturbing as it was, the word also proved to be a new lens with which to see the events of last night. The mystery man had been quite upset when he'd rushed into her shop. Had someone been chasing him? What kind of trouble could he have been in?

Willow either noticed Lou's discomfort or she needed grounding herself after such news, because she put a hand on Lou's arm.

"Where can I get security cameras around here?" Lou asked Detective West.

"I mean, you could order some online, but we have a tech store by the hair salon." He rubbed the back of his neck like he needed a massage, or maybe a vacation. "My buddy Noah could help you with installation if you need it."

"I would really appreciate that," Lou said. Her strengths

lay more in spotting subject/verb agreement issues and plot holes. She could figure out how to install cameras but relaxed in the knowledge she wouldn't have to.

"I can take you to see Noah." Willow stood, checking her watch. "He should be at the shop still, right?" she asked Easton.

He nodded. "I'll let you know if I have any more questions for you, Louisa. I apologize that this happened on your first night in town. It's not much of a welcome, but I'm hoping we can make up for it."

"Thank you, Detective." Lou shook his hand when he held it toward her once more.

With a smile, he stood and grabbed his coat, heading back toward the alley. "Willow, why don't you follow me to the back door, so you can lock it again," he suggested.

Willow did as the detective instructed, but when she returned, she was wrinkling her nose in an expression so sour, it looked like she'd just taken a bite out of a lemon. "Just so you know, he's never that nice," Willow said as she shrugged into her jacket.

Lou kept her mouth shut as she grabbed her own coat from the rack near the front door. Telling Willow how nice Easton seemed would only make her fiery friend more upset. "Who's Noah?" she asked instead. "I've never heard you mention him."

Willow waved a hand. "He's kind of like the local handyman. The man can fix just about everything." She unlocked the door to the bookshop and held it open.

Lou locked it behind them on the way out. The streets had cleared of locals, and only one or two peeked out from nearby businesses. Based on the stories Willow had told over the years about how quickly gossip moved through town, most of them already knew what had happened.

Taking a left, Willow led the way, crossing Thimble Drive. But before they could walk another block, a frantic teenager met up with them.

"Ms. Grey, Oliver did that thing again where he got the pathos all tangled together, and Mrs. Montgomery doesn't know how to fix it." The boy's voice started out deep, but cracked halfway through, jumping to a higher register.

Willow let out a groan. "Okay, Lewis. Tell her I'll be right there." Willow turned to Lou. "I'm so sorry. This will only take a moment to fix."

"I can come with," Lou said.

"Sure, or you could go talk to Noah on your own. He should be right inside there." She motioned toward the store in front of them.

Bolts of fabric were visible through the windows, and gorgeous quilts hung on the walls inside the large shop.

"Material Girls?" Lou asked. The store sat on the corner of Needle and Thread—adorable.

Willow nodded. "Yeah, just go inside. Look for a big, burly guy who seems like he should be chopping down trees in the forest instead of working in a fabric shop. You can't miss him," she called over her shoulder. "I'll be right back." And with that, Willow followed after the high schooler.

Lou stepped forward and pulled open the front door to the quilt shop. Inside, it smelled of fresh cotton, the steam from a hot iron, and that slight vinegar smell all new fabrics hold. Signs hung from the ceiling announcing where to find notions, different fabrics, quilting supplies, and sewing machines. Lou zeroed in on a space near the front of the store that doubled as a cutting counter and register.

Scanning the space for this man she "couldn't miss," Lou noticed three bolts that were in the incorrect section. One of the price signs was slightly askew. Someone had recently brewed a pot of coffee. A group of older women chattered away as they sat around humming sewing machines in the back of the store, but not one of them even glanced over at Lou or seemed concerned about coming to help her.

She was about to walk over to them when a dark-haired man strode out from a back room. He stopped to chat with the women in the sewing machine section. Noah.

Willow had been right. She couldn't miss a burly man like him among the soft fabrics. He wasn't as tall as Detective West, but he seemed bigger. *It must be his shoulders,* Lou thought. He had dark brown hair, a scruffy five o'clock shadow, and thick eyebrows that sat over brown eyes. Despite all the hardness he exuded, there were just as many things about him that spoke of softness. Laugh lines radiated out from the corners of his eyes; he had dimples, and he wore a pastel pink apron.

The moment his gaze caught on Lou, she smiled. It wasn't a normal reaction for her. In New York, people minded their own business. If someone made eye contact, she had looked away more often than not. This person made her want to hold eye contact. His presence made her feel at ease in a way she couldn't qualify.

He strode over to the counter. "Hi there," he said, the dimple on his left cheek deepening even more as he grinned at her. "You must be Louisa."

"Call me Lou." Tilting her head, she added, "How did you know who I was?"

Noah pulled out a phone from his apron pocket and tapped a finger against the side. "Easton texted letting me know you'd be coming by." His dimples disappeared as he pulled his mouth into a frown. "I'm really sorry to hear about what you went through this morning."

His deep voice was calming. Lou let go of the tension in her shoulders. "Thank you."

As someone who'd always been told that she had an innate calming effect on people, it was odd to be on the other side. The sense of calm that surrounded Noah helped her understand the tranquil energy Willow, Ben, and others had described over the years—how she made them feel at ease just being in the same room.

"So you own this place?" Lou asked, surveying the shop. She was immediately glad she'd asked, because Noah's dimpled smile returned.

"Sort of." He squinted one eye as he watched her. "You think that's weird?"

Lou raised her hands to show she didn't have any intention of offending him. "Hey, I'm fine with people having whatever job makes them happy. I mean, I grew up the daughter of a construction supervisor and a kindergarten teacher. My dad is the teacher, and my mom is in construction."

Noah laughed. "I like that." He turned to check on the group of older ladies. "I just have one more thing to finish up before I can help you. Do you want to grab a coffee across the street while you wait and I'll meet you there?"

"That sounds great." Lou had been looking forward to trying out the Bean and Button after all the raving Willow had done about the small coffee shop over the years. She stopped short. "Can I get you something?"

Noah's eyes crinkled. "Sure. I'll take an Americano. Thank you."

Lou nodded and headed out the door toward the shop directly across the street from the bookshop. The Bean and

Button storefront looked very similar to that of her bookstore. The building siding was stained wood, and each window frame was painted a bright collection of colors. Warm yellow lights emitted a glow that only intensified when Lou pulled open the front door.

Sounds spilled out first. The chatter and laughter of people mixed with the banging and grinding sounds of making coffee. Then the smell hit her. Deep notes of bitter coffee combined with the softness of sugar and cream. And then she noticed the buttons. Every surface that could hold them was covered in small plastic covered metal buttons. Some simply said *Button, Wa*. Others held jokes, and some had cartoon pictures.

An old man wearing a bowler cap and fluffy gray eyebrows, sitting at a table to her right, stared at her as she gaped at the décor.

"It's just a lot of buttons," she said in explanation.

"Yeah, well, it ain't called Sticker, so …" He went back to reading his newspaper.

Lou pressed her lips together to hide a smile and stepped forward. She ordered Noah's Americano and a latte for herself. At the last second, she added a scone to the order, realizing she hadn't eaten a thing that morning. Both tables in the front windows were taken, so she found a seat near the back and settled in, reading all the buttons on that section of the wall. Because of the sewing-themed street names, Lou had pictured a shirt button when she thought of the town's name. But she supposed these stick pin buttons worked just as well.

She'd finished her scone and was chuckling at a button that had *Let's Taco Bout It!* written above a cartoon taco when Noah stepped inside the shop and spotted her. He'd exchanged his pink apron for a winter coat but emitted the same softness.

"Ready?" he asked as he approached. "Thank you." He held up the to-go cup as she handed it over.

Lou followed him out of the café. "Where are we going to get this kind of equipment around here?" she asked, eyeing the cutesy candy and ice cream shops.

Noah motioned down the street. Once they'd walked another block, he took a sip of his coffee and nodded to a small building across from them. "George's Technology Emporium."

"Emporium?" Lou repeated, eyeing the building that couldn't have been more than a thousand square feet.

"George has everything." Noah looked both ways and then jogged across the road.

As someone who'd had to pay close attention to car traffic in the city—she'd had a couple near misses with taxis in partic-ular—Lou was awestruck by these small-towners' ability to cross the street with such abandon. Then again, the traffic levels were mere fractions of what she was used to in New York.

George's Technology Emporium smelled like hot plastic and ramen noodles. The space was stacked from floor to ceiling with large plastic bins. In the center of it all was a young woman who appeared to be in her early twenties. She had brown hair twisted into a bun and squished flat under a large headset, complete with a microphone. The chair she occupied was modular, like something out of *Star Trek* rather than a home furnishings store. A video game controller was clutched in her hands, and she was calling out directions into the microphone as she navigated a fantasy-role-playing video game on the large-screen television in front of her.

"We need that troll, everyone. Let's work together," she said into the headset, glancing over at Noah and Lou.

Noah waved as they let the door close behind them. Lou

waited for the young woman to call for her dad, uncle, or grandfather: whoever George was to her.

"Hey guys, I'm out for a bit," she said into her microphone. "Customers."

As she stood and peeled off her headset, Lou studied her sweatshirt. It held a picture of Harrison Ford as Indiana Jones holding a torch forward as he came upon himself as Han Solo, preserved in carbonite, just like in *Star Wars*. It was delightfully thought provoking.

Equally interesting was the way this woman held herself. She stood tall and smiled wide, exhibiting none of the doubt and self-conscious behavior Lou often noticed in young adults, of people who were still trying to figure out who they were.

"Hey Noah," the young woman said. "You here for a security system for the new girl?"

Lou was not only charmed by the fact that this young woman was so self-assured, but also that she'd referred to her —a woman of almost forty—as "the new girl."

"Yep. George, this is Lou." Noah introduced them.

Lou bit back a revelatory inhale. So this was George.

George's face broke out into a wide grin as she noted Lou's surprise. "Lou and George. Don't we make a pair? What's your story? My parents were really into classic literature. *Middlemarch*. You know it?"

"I do." Lou dipped her chin. "My name is actually Louisa, but I go by Lou."

"And you need some cameras, I hear. I set aside some things I think will work." She moved to one of the closest black bins and opened it. Inside was full of electronic gadgets in their original packaging. "I like this set for outside. What do you want inside?" George glanced back at Lou. "Twenty-four-hour coverage or something with a motion sensor?"

"Motion, I think," Lou answered. "I just want it to catch movement if anyone gets inside. I'm not worried about shoplifting." Lou's eyes widened. "Should I be worried about shoplifting?"

George and Noah laughed.

"No. You'll be fine with a motion sensor," George said. "Plus, we can upgrade if you change your mind later."

"Great," Noah said, reaching out to grab the package from George. He studied the back. "This is the same brand I installed for Easton at the police department, right?"

George nodded and brought out an iPad. She poked at the screen for a few seconds before telling Lou the total.

Lou stepped forward, pulling her wallet out of her purse. "Thank you, both of you. I really appreciate your help."

After Lou paid, George handed over a card with her phone number just in case she had any issues. Lou and Noah took the cameras back to the bookshop. As they walked down the block, Lou checked her phone. Willow was probably wondering where she'd gotten to.

She hadn't missed any calls or texts and was about to reach out to Willow when they approached the bookshop, and Lou saw her friend standing among a veritable plant shop.

A dozen potted houseplants sat like waiting customers just outside the front door. But the real surprise was four Japanese magnolia trees in big ceramic pots that Willow had set on either side of the bookshop's front windows. They were blooming, with gorgeous white buds opening to reveal velvety soft flowers.

"Willow," Lou gasped out her friend's name. Her hands covered her mouth, and tears crept into the corners of her eyes. She sniffed, trying to quell the emotion, not wanting to make Noah uncomfortable. "They're beautiful."

"They are. Tragically so," Willow said with a grunt as she moved one back about a foot. "Last week was oddly warm. They got confused. They're not supposed to bloom until next month at the earliest, so these probably won't last long now that we're in another cold snap." Willow shrugged. "Couldn't sell 'em, so you get to enjoy them. You needed something here anyway."

Lou walked forward and pulled her best friend into a hug regardless of how hard the woman tried to pretend it wasn't a big deal.

"You're the best," Lou said before pulling away. "Let me open up, and we can get in out of the cold." Lou stepped carefully over the indoor plants to unlock the shop.

"Perfect, I'm freezing," Willow rubbed her hands together. "Also, I have news. Guess what I heard the police saying when I was setting up those magnolias in the front of the shop?"

Lou slid the key into the lock but turned back toward Willow. Noah tucked the cameras under one arm and grabbed a potted plant in each hand. He watched Willow expectantly, waiting for her to continue.

"The dead man in the alley." Willow motioned to the other side of the building. "All the tags had been cut out of that fancy suit of his."

CHAPTER 4

"What do you mean they were all cut out?" Lou asked Willow as she opened the shop door. Her worried eyes met Noah's equally puzzled ones.

"Someone went in and snipped out the label at the back of the collar and the ones on the inside pockets." Willow shrugged, then picked up two plants.

"Excuse me." A man stopped, looking at Lou as she held open the door. "I'm looking for a few specific used books. You wouldn't happen to have any Bradbury or Salinger?"

Lou smiled. "Oh, I'm sorry. We're not open at the moment. You can check back in a couple of weeks."

The man nodded and kept walking.

"I need to make a sign for the front door," Lou said as Willow and Noah filed inside.

"Back to suit guy," Noah said, setting down the cameras and plants on the check-out counter. "Maybe his mom wrote his name inside his suit like mine used to do on my jackets so I wouldn't lose them at school." He shot them both a playful grin.

But Lou couldn't get past the implications of this move by the killer. "They must've known him."

Willow and Noah waited for her to elaborate.

"In order to know that his suit labels would be enough to identify him, they had to have known him well." Lou chose another potted plant and set it in the middle of the table.

"I'm sure East came to the same conclusion." Noah nodded. He went outside and grabbed the rest of the indoor plants from the sidewalk.

They spent the next few minutes arranging the pots on the windowsills and on bookshelves. The pop of color the house-plants brought was already brightening up the space.

"Is it okay if I get started on those cameras?" Noah asked. "I'll just need to go grab my tools and ladder from my place."

"Of course. I have a ton of work to do in here, so I'll be around. Poke your head in if you need anything." Lou placed the last plant on the check-out counter as Noah left, then turned to Willow. "You should go back to the sale. I've got everything under control here now."

"You sure?" Willow narrowed her eyes.

Lou pushed her toward the door. "Positive. You've already done so much more than I could possibly ask."

Willow laughed as Lou moved her along. "Okay, but I'll check in later."

For the next hour, Lou worked on cleaning. She went upstairs to check on Sapphire, but he was fast asleep on Ben's sweatshirt, the one that Lou had snuggled with last night. She left him alone and went back downstairs to get something else checked off her list while Noah worked outside. Lou had to admit, he was really handy. The man looked very self-assured and capable, standing on a ladder with a tool belt strapped to his waist.

The used-book section of the shop was a bit of a mess, but Lou got that situated quickly. Each book had a sticker on the back cover that listed its price, unless it was in the rare category. Those books contained a bookmark with the title, price, and short blurb explaining why it was considered rare. The shop contained a few first editions and even some signed copies.

As she worked, she catalogued these kinds of things about her new shop. Lou's mind latched on to less important details as well. She knew the mini fridge in the office made a faint clicking noise, a long gash in the wood floor in one corner told a story of a chair with a missing foot, and one section of the shop smelled like Christmas—Lou solved that mystery when she found a cinnamon-soaked pine cone stashed behind a ladder-back chair.

Around noon, Willow stopped by again with sandwiches. All reports coming back from the plant sale were positive, and she was sure they'd surpass their goal.

When Willow offered to help clean, Lou waved her off to go home. She knew Saturdays were usually Willow's guaranteed riding days, when she could get in a good, long workout with her horse.

Besides, now that they lived in the same town, they were going to get to see each other all the time, especially once Lou got the shop up and running. For friends who'd spent the last two decades seeing each other in one year—or two—increments, it was a big deal.

"Kiss OC for me," Lou said, making a mental note to head over to Willow's soon so she could say hello to the horse. It had been almost three years since she'd seen him last.

OC was short for Of Course. Willow had watched a lot of reruns of the show *Mr. Ed* when she was growing up, and so when she'd purchased a spunky chestnut foal from a local breeder five years ago, and Lou had asked what his name would be, she'd sung the first line of the *Mr. Ed* theme song, "A horse is a horse, of course, of course." One of Willow's favorite things was explaining his name to people who asked.

"I will." Willow waved goodbye.

Tired of cleaning, Lou turned her attention to inventory for a while. She was confident she could teach herself the ins and outs of the inventory software. She was just loading it on the register computer a few minutes later when Noah stepped inside.

He held his phone in one hand. "I have something I need to take care of," he said, shaking the phone in the air. "I'll be back in a few hours. I'm done outside. I just have to link them all and do the digital setup. I can hang the one inside for you when I get back."

Lou replied that it all sounded great. The man was doing her such a big favor. After he left, she locked the front door and then checked her purse for cash to make sure she had enough to pay him for his help.

Lou turned on some soothing music, knowing she needed to concentrate. When she used to edit, she preferred listening to harp or piano music, maybe light jazz. Nothing that would distract her too much. She put on Ben's favorite jazz pianist and situated herself behind the computer.

By the time Noah returned, the sun had set, and Lou felt like the master of her inventory system. She'd had to troubleshoot a little—and watch a handful of videos to help her figure out certain functions—but she could now enter a book, remove a title, and knew how to use the program with her sales software.

"Nice music," Noah said with a curious smile. "I guess I

shouldn't be surprised that a New Yorker has good taste in jazz, huh?"

Lou was about to ask how he'd known she was from New York when she remembered she now lived in a small town. Her moving in from the city was likely big news.

"Everything work out okay?" she asked, remaining vague. He hadn't offered any details about what it was he'd left to take care of, so she didn't want to pry.

He nodded. "All good." Scanning the room, he asked, "Now, where are you thinking for the interior camera?"

Lou surveyed the space up toward the ceiling, where they would get the best view. "What about up here?" She pointed to the corner behind the register. From that angle, the shot should include the entire shop.

"That should work." Noah squinted as he seemed to make calculations in his mind. "Since you mentioned you don't need it for theft prevention, we can block out business hours so it's not recording throughout the day."

Picking up her cleaning supplies again, Lou agreed. "If you give me an hour buffer on either side, that would be great, so I don't trip it when I'm doing opening or closing duties either."

Noah went to get his ladder from outside and was teetering up near the ceiling just a few minutes later. "Okay, I think we're all set here." He wiped his hands on his jeans and climbed down.

"Thank you, so much." Lou hadn't realized how much the security was worrying her until that moment. A weight lifted off her chest.

Settling at the table, Noah pulled out instruction booklets and motioned for her to join him. He instructed her to download a certain app and then showed her how to sync the cameras.

"You'll probably want to write your password down somewhere, just in case," he told her. His eyes swept across the table. "Can I use this paper?" he asked, picking up a cream-colored book page.

Lou frowned. "What is that?"

"It was just here." He gestured with the paper to show where it had been tucked under the corner of the stack of books Sapphire had napped on yesterday. "Someone already wrote on it, so I thought you were using it for notes." Noah held it out to Lou so she could get a better look.

The size and texture of the page made it obvious that it had been taken from a book. She sucked in a sharp inhale.

"The man who I found dead in the alley this morning was carrying a book page in his hand when he rushed in yesterday. He sat at this table." Lou flipped the paper over and then back again. "I didn't see him leave, so I just figured he'd taken it with him ..."

"But if he ran out, maybe he left it behind," Noah finished the thought for her.

Intrigued, they inspected the paper. On one side, notes were scrawled upon the page in pen.

> Harriet - ~~Anne of Green Gables~~
> Gerald - ~~The Catcher in the Rye~~, Asimov?
> Tonya - Stephen King?
> Bethany - ~~The Wizard of Oz~~
> Jessamyn - Olivia Queen?

Turning over the page, there was a standard dedication centered in the blank space.

Charlie, in the Queen household, you'll always be king. - Olivia

Noah sniffed, dismissing it. But Lou couldn't. A tightness pulled at her shoulder blades, and she sat up straight in alarm. Something wasn't right.

"What is it?" Noah asked, catching onto her nonverbal cues.

"Olivia Queen was one of my authors," she said, then tore her gaze away from the page to meet Noah's eyes. "That's what I did in New York. I was an editor. Olivia was the first author I discovered."

Noah let out a low whistle. "She's a pretty big deal."

Lou nodded and pointed to the dedication page. "Her husband's name is Charles."

"So this is the dedication page from one of her books?" Noah asked. The frown lines forming in between his eyebrows proved he wasn't understanding why this was a big deal.

Lou swallowed. "The thing is, it couldn't be. During the final stages of her first book, I was trying to help her with her dedication and was just throwing out suggestions. Olivia turned down my idea to dedicate the book to her husband. She said he'd asked her never to do that—he was really shy, you see—and she wanted to respect his wishes."

"Maybe he changed his mind, now that you've left," Noah suggested.

Olivia had turned in a book right around the time Ben died. Lou had handed it off to another editor, apologizing to Olivia, but letting her know she just couldn't handle it. So that was a possibility. Then again, it really wasn't.

"She called him Chuck, rarely Charles, and never Charlie." Lou cut the air with her hand. "This can't be real."

Confusion roiled around Lou, like steam bubbling off a pot of boiling water.

"I think Easton needs to see this. It could help him in the

investigation." Noah pulled out his phone.

"Right. Absolutely," Lou said, but her phone stole away her attention when it lit up with a notification. "Oh," she said with surprise. "I have my first camera alert."

Opening the app and pressing the button to go to the live feed, she expected to pull up the camera and find a stray cat, or maybe an alley raccoon waddling by. But an icy fear dripped down her spine as she focused on the black-and-white night-vision feed her phone projected. A person dressed in dark colors, wearing a hood and a knit cap pulled low over their forehead, snuck toward her back door.

Noah stopped the message he was typing to Easton and leaned closer, watching the feed with her. The figure studied the building for a few seconds before trying the door. Noah and Lou's attention shot to the back of the shop where they heard the door handle jiggle. Noah jumped up from his seat and jogged toward the back.

"They're leaving," she called as the figure darted away. "Fast."

In the video, the door opened. Noah rushed out into the alley. He searched right, then left, and along each side of the building, but came back a moment later.

"They were quick." Lou shook her head, showing Noah he wouldn't have been able to catch them even if he'd been faster.

Noah grabbed his phone and held it to his ear. A dial tone rang out in the quiet space as he waited. "Easton, can you come to the bookstore?" There was a pause as Noah listened to his response. "Thanks. We found something you might need, and a person just tried to get in through the back door."

As Lou listened, the ache of foreboding dread started in her chest. She contemplated the confusing book page in her hands and noticed her fingers were shaking.

CHAPTER 5

Easton paced through the bookshop. He'd seen the video footage, had studied the odd dedication page, and was currently shaking his head.

"None of it makes sense," he said. "I don't think it will until we figure out the identity of our victim."

"Could Lou be in danger?" Noah asked, his jaw clenching tight as he glanced over at her.

Easton ran his fingers through his sandy brown hair. "No. Local news ran the story about the body in the alley during the evening segment about an hour prior to your visitor. I bet it's just one of those morbidly curious people checking out the alley. We got everything we could from the scene, so it's okay if people go back there."

"The news mentioned my bookshop?" Lou asked, concern edging her tone.

Easton gave her an apologetic grimace. "I know it's not ideal, but in cases like this, knowing the location can sometimes help us with the identity. We also gave them a sketch of the victim, so we'll see if any tips come in, or if anyone knows who our mystery man is."

Noah appeared about as convinced as Lou felt. "Maybe you shouldn't stay here tonight," he suggested.

Lou chewed on her lip as she contemplated the idea. Willow *had* said she was welcome anytime. Maybe she should take her friend up on the offer. The only problem was, Lou didn't have a way to get there. Living in New York, she and Ben had never needed a car. Now that she lived in a rural town, she knew it was something she would have to purchase. She just hadn't gotten around to it yet.

"I can drop you by Willow's on my way home," Easton said, as if he were reading her mind. "She mentioned you're without a car at the moment."

Lou nodded. "Thank you. Let me get my cat and a few things for overnight."

The men told her to take her time, and she ran upstairs to pack while they waited. She texted Willow a heads-up and packed a bag. Sapphire was not thrilled to go back in his crate, but if there were murderers lurking around the building, she was not about to leave him here alone. She checked her phone again but still hadn't gotten a response from Willow. It wasn't unusual. Willow didn't always take her phone with her when she was out back working with OC.

Before she could put her phone away, another notification showed up on her screen from the security system. Lou's breath felt stuck in her throat. Was the lurker back? But as she opened the app and pressed the live-feed button, she realized it was showing her the inside of the bookshop. It was far past business hours, and Noah or Easton must've set it off. The feed showed Easton settling into a seat at the table next to Noah.

"You have any plans for tonight?" he asked.

Noah smiled. Even through the grainy black-and-white video, Lou swore she could see those dimples. "Just pizza and a movie with Marigold."

Easton nodded. "Nice."

Lou closed the app, suddenly feeling like she was spying on them, listening in on a conversation not meant for her. She grabbed her bag, picked up Sapph's crate, and shuffled back down the stairs. The men stood as she walked over.

Noah bent forward to get a better look at Sapphire. "He has beautiful eyes," he said, booping the cat's nose with his finger as Sapph smelled him through the metal door.

"Thanks. He's a pretty special guy." Lou held him closer.

"Deaf?" Noah asked, glancing from the cat to her.

"He is," Lou confirmed.

Easton twirled his keys. "Ready?"

Lou followed him outside to a dark sedan. "Thank you so much, Noah." She turned back after setting Sapphy's crate in the back seat of Easton's car. "How much do I owe you for your help?" She pulled out her wallet.

Noah waved a hand and said, "That was on me. Take it as a Welcome to Button gift." He coughed. "To combat the less-than-ideal first impression you got of us."

She thought about offering dinner, but now that she'd heard him talk about Marigold, that idea didn't seem smart. Even if she was just looking for friendship, she didn't want anyone to get the wrong impression.

"Well, thank you," Lou said, vowing to return the favor someday.

Easton drove her out to Spool Avenue, just a few miles down the road. It was much more rural than the downtown section where Lou lived. Houses sat on larger plots of land, some closer to an acre, others more. He pulled up the long driveway he and Willow shared, taking the left up to her place.

"Thanks for the ride." Lou opened the door.

"Anytime." Easton waved. "And don't worry too much about that lurker. If you see anything else that worries you, call me. Do you want my number?"

"I can get it from Willow." Lou scooted out of the car and grabbed Sapph and her bag out of the back seat.

Easton gave her a salute as she closed the door, then he backed up about a hundred feet and turned right into his driveway.

Willow's home was a cute, sage-green farmhouse. In contrast to Easton's immaculate gray house with perfect land-scaping and one decoration—a carved wooden bear holding a welcome sign that appeared to be kept on his porch year-round—Willow's house was lived in and loved. It was like the difference between a comfy worn-in chair and the flashy, uncomfortable kind on display in pristine furniture showrooms.

Lou knocked on the front door and waited. There was no answer.

She pulled out her key ring and unlocked the door herself. Three years ago, when Willow had purchased the house and had given Lou her own key, it was purely symbolic. But now that they lived close by, Lou knew she was just as welcome in Willow's house as Willow was in the bookshop or in Lou's apartment.

Which reminds me: I need to get some copies made of the book-shop keys and give those to Willow, Lou mused as she let herself inside.

The interior of the house was the purest reflection of Lou's best friend she could imagine. Plants were everywhere. If someone didn't know Willow and walked inside, they might wonder if the inhabitant of the house had a compulsive plant-buying problem—it was *that* many plants. But Lou knew that half of them were being rehabbed in order to be returned to the school greenhouse, and another quarter of them most likely belonged to friends and coworkers who'd given up hope. Willow would nurse them back to health and return them to their former owners, good as new—or better.

Other than that, she'd decorated the place in cozy neutrals and functional pieces. Lou moved around a comfy sofa and set down Sapphy's crate. She opened the door to let him out but left it open so he could access the litter box in the back, along with food and water. Lou was even more grateful for the purchase. It had come in handy so many times already on their cross-country journey.

Once the cat had slunk out and was curled up on Willow's sofa, Lou exited through the back door toward the small barn. Willow owned an acre and a half. On that land, she had a paddock, round pen, and arena where she worked OC. During the weekends, she let him graze on the grassy area in between the paddock and the house. She had to be careful, though, because those were the occasions the horse got into the most mischief, namely into Easton's yard.

From what Willow had described to Lou over the years, Easton was a pretty big gardener himself. In the moonlight, Lou could see a few raised beds full of vegetables in his yard. The small fence in between the two yards wouldn't phase OC at all. In fact, Willow had described how it only took a short reach of his long neck to snack on peas, broccoli, and a myriad of lettuces, much to Easton's chagrin.

It wasn't as if Willow dismissed OC's thieving ways. She knew what it was like to grow something she was proud of and didn't want to increase the strife between her and her neighbor. She'd tried everything to keep OC out, but even when she kept him confined to the paddock area, he found a way through and would have his head buried in that vegetable patch within minutes of his escape.

A warm light glowed from the small barn in the deepening darkness, acting as a beacon to Lou. A soft snort and the stamp of a hoof told Lou she was headed in the right direction. But before she could enter the barn, a small, light gray goat galloped into the entrance, blocking her path.

"Oh. Hello." Lou stopped and regarded the little creature. He was wearing … blue pajamas. She reached down to pet him.

When her hand was within a foot of the goat, the animal opened its mouth and let out the loudest, most scream-like sound she'd ever encountered. It was so alarming that Lou staggered back a few feet.

"Steve? What are you screaming at?" Willow's voice came from inside.

Steve? Lou bit back a laugh. "He's yelling at me," she called out. "I think you have a guard goat here. He won't let me in."

Willow appeared a second later. "Hey. Sorry. This is Steve. I just got him last week."

"Because you needed someone to defend the barn?" Lou guessed.

Laughing, Willow said, "I thought OC needed a friend. I hoped that if he had something to entertain him, he wouldn't spend so much energy trying to escape next door." She scooped up Steve and patted his wiry little head.

Lou reached forward and petted him. "Has it worked?"

"So far …" Willow's chin dropped. "No. In fact, he's taught

OC a bunch of new, mischievous tricks." She huffed out an exasperated exhale. "But he sure is cute."

"He definitely is." Lou followed Willow as she turned and headed inside.

The barn was small, with space for a tack room, a hay storage alcove, and two stalls that opened out into the paddock, but it was cozy. OC stood in the walkway between the tack room and the stalls, clipped into crossties. Willow must've been at the end of her grooming routine because his chestnut coat shone even through all the winter fluff.

The enormous horse stamped his right hoof and bobbed his head up and down at the sight of Lou. At close to seventeen hands, he was the perfect size for a tall person like Willow, but a little intimidating for someone Lou's height. Willow had once remarked that being around horses was the first time she felt small in her life.

Lou strode up to OC, holding out her hand. She would've been intimidated by the large animal if she hadn't known him since he was a foal. She'd spent a week with Willow when she'd first gotten him and had helped with the feedings and halter training. So even though he weighed the better part of a ton now, he was still that tiny little guy in her heart, all long, tangly legs with a whinny so high-pitched it made them burst into laughter each time they heard it.

"Hi, big guy. It's been a while, huh?" Lou took another slow step forward.

OC snuffled his velvety nose into Lou's open palm, moving his lip back and forth in search of a treat. She moved her hand up to hold on to his halter and pressed her forehead into his. He pushed his nose into her affectionately.

"You can grab a carrot. This boy deserves all the treats today. He successfully did two flying changes in a row."

Willow set down the goat and started packing up her grooming supplies.

Lou scratched around OC's ears, one of his favorite spots. "Good job, buddy." She moved to a feed bin that held oats and supplements, and fished a carrot out of a bag. OC chomped happily, chewing with such joyous abandon that the macerated carrot foamed and flicked out of his mouth.

Steve scampered over and chomped on the larger pieces the horse dropped.

"Why pajamas?" Lou asked, admiring the cute little creature.

Willow shrugged. "Why not?"

Lou laughed. "Fair point."

"You get tired of cleaning and unpacking?" Willow asked as she set the currycomb in the grooming caddy. "Not that I'm unhappy to see you. I just didn't think you were coming over tonight."

Lou inhaled, holding the air in her lungs for a moment. "I didn't either," she said after she exhaled. She explained about the piece of paper Noah had found from the mystery man and the shady figure that had come to the shop's back door.

Willow wiggled out a shiver. "That's creepy. I'm glad you're staying here tonight. I think Easton might be right, though. It's probably just lookie-loos coming around to see the scene of the crime after that story on the news tonight."

"You saw it?" Lou wrinkled her nose. "So they really mentioned Button Books?"

"Yeah, not the best publicity, huh?"

Lou leaned into OC's muscular neck, reveling in his warmth. "Maybe it'll attract the mystery-reading crowd. Who knows? All I know is that this whole situation seems like a lot of stress and drama."

"Two things you definitely don't need right now," Willow agreed.

And even though she felt better after talking to her friend, Lou had a terrible feeling her problems weren't over. The possibility sat in her mind like a gloomy cloud on the horizon.

CHAPTER 6

Lou and Willow spent Sunday morning lazily sipping coffee and making waffles for a leisurely brunch. Fortunately, Lou didn't get any more security camera notifications showing disturbing lurkers around the shop.

It was just after noon when Lou decided to return to the bookshop. "I think you and Easton are right. That person last night must've just been curious about the crime scene," she said when Willow asked if she was sure.

Willow squished soapy water from a sponge as she washed their breakfast dishes. "Okay, well come on back if you feel at all weird tonight. Or I could come stay with you."

Lou contemplated the idea. As tempting as it sounded, she needed to be comfortable on her own. Plus, Willow had work early tomorrow morning, and Lou didn't want to disturb her morning routine.

"I'll let you know," she said noncommittally, "but I think it's kind of like how you have to get right back on OC each time you fall off. I need to get back in there by myself to prove my fears are unwarranted. Thanks for the offer, though, and breakfast."

Willow wiped her hands on a dish towel. "Anytime. Let me help you pack up."

When Lou stepped through the bookshop door with Sapphire less than thirty minutes later, she knew it had been the right decision to come back. The plants Willow had gifted her had already improved both the musty smell and the dingy appearance of the bookstore. But the most important thing was that Lou got a warm, fuzzy feeling as she entered, just like she used to when she visited this shop as a customer during her trips to visit Willow. Doubt and apprehension must've crowded the feeling when she'd set foot inside for the first time. But there it was.

The events of yesterday had made Lou question her decision to buy the shop, more than once. She'd been worried she'd made a mistake by quitting her job and moving away from the city. But that butterfly feeling of happiness she felt now made it all worth it.

Motivated, Lou focused on getting her apartment space squared away. She took Sapphire upstairs and emptied all the kitchen boxes. After giving the cupboards and countertops a thorough cleaning, she put everything in its new place.

Then she started on the boxes of clothing she'd pushed aside her first night there. At the bottom of the first one, she found her running shoes. Glancing back at the dresser, where she'd just seen a sports bra and running pants, she decided it was the perfect time for a run. Checking the weather outside the window, she ascertained that it would be chilly but sunny.

She changed, stuffed a key into the secret pocket hidden in her running pants, and headed out the door. The winter air stung at her ears immediately as she stretched in front of the bookstore. Once she'd warmed up a bit, she took a left and ran up Thimble Drive. She was glad she'd found her fleece headband in the moving boxes and tugged it lower to cover her ears completely.

While Ben had been one to listen to music or audiobooks as he ran, Lou liked to listen to the surrounding sounds: the wind rustling the leaves, the sound of her shoes crunching along the pavement, the rhythm of her breathing, and the birds in the trees. This turned out to be even more pleasant in a small town. She smiled at the friendly greetings of the locals as they walked by one another, waved at those who raised a hand in greeting toward her, and made mental notes of the places she wanted to come back to visit.

The Button Boutique was in the building behind her. From the glimpse she got through their window as she passed, their clothes appeared to be both cozy and cute. She'd have to visit another day to grab a few new items. Taking a left at the corner to run along Spool Avenue, she passed by the Button Beer and BBQ building, knowing Willow often talked about going to the *Three Bs,* as she and the other locals called it. She couldn't wait to try their food.

Farther down Spool Avenue, Lou passed the Button Bistro and a children's clothing store. Lou waited for a car to pass and then crossed Spool Avenue so she could take a right on Binding Street. As she ran, she noticed the high school track and middle school on her right. On her left, the businesses gave way to a cute pond and residential streets.

The houses were just as adorable as the downtown business buildings. They were painted in muted Easter egg colors, and each held an adorable front garden that seemed to change based on the personality of the resident. She took a left on Pattern Drive, looping down through the neighborhood. She crossed Spool Avenue and took a right to run farther down Thread Lane. Lou frowned as she spotted a giant house across the street, hidden behind overgrown trees and brush. The building had three stories and peeling gables.

Unlike the other houses lined up in neighborhoods, this home was alone on a wooded plot of land. It was unkempt and dilapidated, appearing to be uninhabited. It was the only house that didn't have a front garden. In fact, the house seemed to hide behind a row of bamboo planted along the street. She couldn't seem to look away as she jogged forward. Intrigue wore off as Lou passed by Willow's house, waving to OC in his paddock.

Her breath settled into a steady rhythm. Three counts in, two counts out. The close-set houses gave way to larger parcels. With less to inspect, Lou let her mind wander as she ran by the fields. Her thoughts returned to the poor man in the suit, how she'd found him slumped against the building. Then her memory brought back the picture of Ben, sitting against the trunk of a tree, like he was taking a break, about to get back up. Only he never had.

The memories of that day floated through Lou's thoughts so often, it sometimes seemed as if she would never rid herself of them.

Ben had gone on a run like he always did on Saturday mornings. When an hour passed by and he hadn't returned, Lou grew anxious. He'd had the same route and pace for the last ten years. It never took him longer than forty minutes.

She called his phone, only to find he'd left it behind. Donning her own running shoes, Lou had gone out to search his normal route through Central Park. Instead of the measured breathing she employed during jogs—three counts in, two counts out—her breath had come in frantic gasps.

She must've been the picture of panic because a young woman had run up to her, asking if she was looking for a man with a dark beard and bright green shoes. Yes! Yes, that was her husband. Relief washed over her. She wanted to laugh. Benjamin and his garish running shoes.

When Lou nodded, the hope that sprang forward at the person's description was suddenly knocked back on its heels. Because the stranger's expression hadn't lit up like Lou's. In fact, it grew even more grim.

She placed a steadying hand on Lou's arm as she led her over to a place off the trail. It deviated from his regular path enough that Lou wouldn't have searched there if it hadn't been for the woman. EMTs crowded the scene.

That moment had been the very worst of Lou's entire life.

It had been the exact time she'd known. All of her worries from the past hour had come true. He was gone.

She followed numbly as the woman explained that she'd been reading on a bench as Ben had run past. It wasn't until he'd looped around that she noticed how sick he seemed, how he was staggering to a stop and grasping at his chest. The woman had run to his aid, calling 9-1-1 immediately.

But it had been too late.

She'd helped him to the ground, leaning him back against the trunk of a tree, which was where Lou found him as she and the woman approached.

"I found his wife, I think," the woman had announced to the paramedics. "He didn't have any identification on him, so we were worried we wouldn't be able to find his family," she'd explained to Lou. "I've been wandering through the park looking for people who might be missing someone."

In a daze, Lou had thanked the woman for sticking around. The paramedics explained how he'd suffered from a heart attack during his run. These things happened, even to people as healthy as him. They delicately outlined what would happen next for her. Lou remembered all of it with such precision, but at the same time, wasn't sure how well she could recall any of it.

Now, as she ran past a field occupied by two fluffy horses in winter blankets, she noticed her breath had become ragged all over again, just as it had that day almost a year ago. She stopped on the side of the road, settling her hands on her knees and pulling in deep, icy breaths. The air wheezed in and out of her lungs, and she coughed as the cold bit into her chest, and tears crowded her eyes.

The first few times she'd gone running after Ben's death, these coughing fits had always turned into sobs, huge emotional releases that found her sitting on the side of the running trail to cry it all out. It was expected that this move would trigger more big emotions.

But just as Lou felt hot tears stream down her cheeks, she heard something that made her swipe them away. A small meow had come from the bush to Lou's right.

"Hello?" she called, swiping at her face as she stepped forward.

The mew came again, this time closer. Lou pushed aside a branch as she peered closer into the rhododendron bush. A tiny orange kitten came rushing forward, meowing one long, distraught sound like it was afraid Lou would leave if it didn't keep making noise.

"Whoa, what are you doing all the way out here, little one?" She scooped up the cat as it practically jumped at her through the branches.

The kitten purred as if its life depended on it, rubbing against Lou's hands, neck, and chin. It was frighteningly cold to the touch. She held it away from her body for a moment, unzipping her jacket about halfway. While she held the cat in front of her, she inspected the tiny creature for any wounds. Its right ear was ripped a bit at the top, and a small amount of blood clung to the cut, but other than that, she couldn't find any other obvious injuries.

Gently setting the kitten inside her jacket, she zipped it back up and kept one hand cradled underneath its body so it wouldn't slip out the bottom of her jacket. Right away, it curled into a ball and settled in for a nap, small paws kneading happily against her stomach.

"Okay, little one. Let's see. Where did you come from?" Satisfied that it would be warmer now, she scanned her surroundings for clues about where it came from. The bush it'd been hiding under was next to a fence near the road. The closest house was at least a mile away on either side of the road. She didn't see any signs of other kittens or a mother in the nearby bushes or field.

The kitten was alone.

Lou sighed, peeking into her jacket to find it fast asleep, purring up a storm. She chuckled, then turned around, facing back the way she'd come. She wasn't more than a mile from home. Walking this time instead of running, she headed back.

When she returned, she set her key on the table in the bookshop before carefully unzipping her jacket. The kitten blinked awake, eyes instantly wide as it took in its new surroundings. Lou pulled out her phone and searched for a local veterinarian.

"I think we need to get you checked out and see if anyone knows who you belong to," Lou told the kitten as the search results populated her screen. "Oh good. The Button Veterinary

Clinic is just a couple blocks away," she explained to the creature as it sniffed the contents of the table.

Before she even noticed he'd come over, Sapphire vaulted up onto the table next to Lou, the hair on his back standing up as he regarded the kitten. Lou stiffened.

"Sapphy, I'm sorry. This little one was in trouble, and I had to bring him inside." She moved to grab her cat off the table, but paused as the orange kitten noticed the older cat.

Just as it had when it had spotted Lou, the kitten raced forward, mouth open in a desperate meow. Sapphy froze as the kitten approached, but relaxed when it rubbed up against his body, purring away once more.

"I think it likes you," Lou said with a laugh.

Sapph seemed to return the compliment. After a moment's hesitation, he cleaned the kitten's head and purred to match the kitten's intensity.

"I hate to break this up, but we need to find out who this little one belongs to." Lou scooped the kitten back into her arms.

She grabbed Sapph's travel carrier and settled the kitten inside before heading out the door to make the trip to the veterinary clinic. The website said they were open for a couple more hours, so she wanted to make sure she caught them before they went home for the day.

Crossing Thread Lane, she realized the clinic was located just behind the coffee shop. A receptionist looked up from behind a desk as Lou entered. The woman was older and had her graying hair pulled back into a braid. Her kind, brown eyes wrinkled at the corners as she took in Lou and the cat carrier she held at her side.

"Welcome, and who do we have here?" The woman stood so she could get a better view inside the crate.

"I'm not sure, actually," Lou said.

The woman's eyes flicked up to her in question.

"I found this kitten on the side of the road while I was on a run just now. It has a cut on its ear, but doesn't seem to be hurt beyond that. Could someone here check to see if its microchipped? I'd hate to think someone's missing it. I just couldn't leave it out there in the cold."

The woman nodded emphatically as Lou described the situation. "Of course. Of course," she said, settling back into her chair and squinting at her computer screen. "The doctor is just finishing up an exam, and should be done shortly. I'll fit you in right after that." She peered at Lou for a moment. "You're the newcomer, right? Bought the bookshop?"

Lou smiled. "Yes. You can call me Lou."

Holding a hand to her chest, the woman said, "I'm Kathleen. Lovely to meet you." She motioned to a row of chairs along the front wall. "You can wait over there. I'll call you over when we're ready."

Lou sat, settling the crate gently in between her feet. The kitten crunched away at the food she'd put inside, and she could hear the faint lapping of water.

"Just a shame about what happened to that poor man in your alleyway, isn't it?" Kathleen said from across the waiting room.

"It was awful," Lou agreed.

"Our Easton is the best around. He'll figure out what happened in no time. Don't you worry," Kathleen added just as the exam room door opened.

An old golden retriever on a leash ambled out, panting heavily as it pulled its owner toward the door. The man on the other end of the leash laughed, saying, "Hold on, Murph.

We've gotta pay first." He steered the dog toward Kathleen's desk and it lay in a heap at his feet.

Kathleen and the man with the golden retriever talked about payment, but Lou didn't hear much of it, because the man who stepped out of the exam room behind him, dressed in scrubs and a white lab coat, was someone she knew.

"Noah?" she asked, getting to her feet.

CHAPTER 7

Noah's dimpled smile widened as he focused on Lou. "Hey," he said, tipping his head in surprised welcome.

"You're a vet?" she asked, eyeing his white lab coat with *Dr. Ramero* stitched above the breast pocket. "I thought you owned the quilt shop." She motioned toward Material Girls. "And installed security systems in people's businesses."

Noah laughed. "I guess it sounds like a lot when you put it like that. This is my primary job. My family owns the quilt shop and I help from time to time. Is something wrong with your cat?" he asked, glancing down at the crate by her feet.

Lou blinked as she tried to remember why she was here. Seeing Noah so unexpectedly had thrown her off-balance.

"She found a kitten on the side of the road," Kathleen answered for her. The man with the golden retriever was leaving, and Kathleen came out from behind the reception desk. "I told her you might have a minute to examine it before you finish up for the day," she said.

Noah nodded. "Of course. Bring it in here." He turned around, reentering the exam room.

Lou picked up the crate and followed. "Thank you so much." She set the crate on the stainless steel exam table inside. "I was on a run out by the big farm on Thread Lane when I heard it mewing away in a bush. It practically jumped into my arms."

Noah listened, opening up the crate door and peeking inside.

"It tore its ear, and I wanted to make sure it doesn't have any other injuries." Lou stood back as Noah extracted the kitten. It purred and rubbed its small face against his hands. "And I wasn't sure if you could check to see if it's microchipped."

"We sure can." Noah tsked as he examined the torn ear and set the kitten on the counter. He did a few more quick examinations, peeking inside the ears, checking the kitten's teeth, and palpating its stomach before picking it back up. "It's a very lucky thing you found this little guy. I don't think he would've made it outside much longer in the cold with this short coat. I'm going to steal him away to the back room for a moment. We'll be right back."

Him. It's a little boy kitten, Lou mused as she took a seat in the corner while she waited for Noah and the kitten to return.

More than a few minutes passed, and Lou wished she'd brought a book with her. Instead, she busied herself by reading the different informational posters Noah had up in the exam room. She could name all the parts of a cat's digestive system and the dangers of ticks by the time he returned with the kitten.

"Kathleen and my vet tech are officially in love with him," Noah said with a laugh. "This guy is a heartbreaker, but he is not microchipped. And other than this cut on his ear, he seems in good health. I gave him his kitten shots and got a sample from him. He doesn't have any parasites, which is rare coming off the street like this." Noah set the kitten on the counter. His orange fur was damp and his ear was clean. "I gave him a quick flea bath," Noah explained.

"Thank you." Lou's mind wandered as she wondered what it meant that the little guy wasn't microchipped.

"What would you like to do next?" Noah asked. "You could keep him, of course, but I don't want you to feel you have to."

"Keep him?" Lou hadn't really thought about having another cat besides Sapphy.

"I can call Barb before I leave and see if she has space to foster him until we find him a home." He scratched the kitten's head.

Lou stood. "Oh, a foster?" The thought of committing to another cat for the rest of its life right now sounded overwhelming, but she liked the idea of fostering. She didn't want to say goodbye to the little guy just yet. "I could foster him."

This is it, Lou realized. *This is how I can help repay Noah. I can take care of this little guy until he finds a permanent home.*

"Are you sure?" Noah narrowed his eyes at her.

She nodded. "Absolutely. How hard can it be to find a home for an adorable little kitten? Plus, he already gets along with my cat. They met before I brought him here."

Noah placed his hands on the exam table. "Well, that solves that problem, then." His eyes crinkled as he smiled. "Can I send you home with some food and litter? We get samples from vendors."

"Sure. I'd also love to get him some toys. There's a pet store in town, right?" she asked with a cringe, realizing she still had a lot to learn about her new home.

Noah laughed. "Yes, a couple blocks over on Binding Street, across from the furniture store," he said as he walked her out to the reception desk.

Before she left, they made another appointment for the kitten's second round of shots. She insisted on paying for the visit, much to Kathleen's chagrin, but knew this was yet another way she could thank Noah for his help yesterday.

WHEN SHE ARRIVED BACK at the bookshop, people crowded in front of the store. They scattered as she walked up to the door, but not without whispering and glancing over their shoulders at her.

Lou rarely gave much mental energy to what other people thought of her. As an editor, there was always someone who didn't agree with her. It came as no surprise with a job that consisted of so much constructive criticism. But the finished product always spoke of her abilities, as did the authors who loved working with her once they saw what she could do for their books.

Running a bookshop was a whole different story, she realized. Image mattered, and the image being projected to the town and its tourists about Button Books wasn't favorable.

Heading inside and locking the door behind her, Lou contemplated this. She took a few moments to show the kitten where the litter box, food, and water were located, and then set him free. She worked on inputting the books in stock into her inventory software. It was a mindless task she could knock off her list while monitoring the kitten.

When Lou and Ben had adopted a baby Sapphire years ago, they'd endured weeks of what they called *velcro kitten*. Tiny, white Sapphy hurled his body everywhere and climbed everything in sight, even their legs sometimes. Lou regarded the little orange cat, waiting for him to claw at the wrong thing or zip across the shop, but he just curled up in a ball next to a sleeping Sapphy.

He'd had a long day. Lou gazed fondly at the napping cats.

Outside the front windows, she noticed another group of onlookers whispering and frowning at the building. She needed to do something about the bad press. Her unopened status only seemed to hurt the cause. If her doors had been open during this whole ordeal, she could welcome customers inside and show them how warm and inviting the shop could be. But the place was far from cozy or ready, and all they saw from the outside were dusty, sparse shelves in a dark shop.

Lou called Willow, hoping hearing her friend's voice might rescue her from the negative headspace she was in.

"Hey. How's everything going?" Willow asked cheerily.

"I found a kitten on my run today. I also learned that Noah's the local vet, Button's handyman, and part owner of Material Girls." Lou recounted the list of things that had transpired in the hours since she left her friend.

"Yeah, like I said, he fixes stuff around here." Willow snorted out a laugh.

Lou rolled her eyes at herself. She should've known better than to take Willow's words at face value. Willow had always had a fluid relationship with the truth. In fact, it was how they'd become friends all those decades ago.

It had been the first month of second grade, and Lou had just gotten into the Ramona books. She couldn't stop reading them—even when she was supposed to be paying close attention to a math lesson. When Mrs. Miller called on Lou for the answer to a question she hadn't heard, Lou knew she was going to get a phone call home. In hindsight, the punishment didn't seem like that big of a deal, but to seven-year-old Lou, the thought was devastating.

Before Lou could pull the book out of her desk to show her teacher, Willow had spoken up from the next seat over.

"I'm sorry, Mrs. Miller. It was my fault."

"Your fault?" Mrs. Miller had asked, putting a hand on her hip.

"I asked Lou a question." Second-grade Willow had been lithe and fairylike, as if she'd just wandered in from the forest.

Mrs. Miller had given her best stern-teacher look, but Lou hadn't missed the slight smile that pulled at the corners of the woman's lips. She, and everyone else around, couldn't help but be charmed by the charismatic child.

"Thank you for being honest, Willow. Next time, raise your hand and ask your question to the entire class instead of just Lou. If you're having a hard time with a math problem, there's a chance others are as well, and we can all learn together." Mrs. Miller turned back to the board.

Lou had let out the biggest sigh of relief. Willow had patted her on her shoulder and said, "Don't worry."

They'd been best friends ever since.

"So you found a kitten. Are you keeping it?" Willow asked, a teasing trill to her question.

"Just until I find someone to adopt him. He's super sweet and adorable, so I'm sure that won't be long." Lou gazed fondly at the orange ball of fluff.

"A real Romeow," Willow said.

Lou laughed. "Actually, he is. Had everyone in Noah's

office wrapped around his little paw." Lou shook her head. "I think I have to call him Romeow now. It's too cute."

"I think you do. So … what's up?" Willow asked, sensing there was an underlying reason behind the call.

"You mentioned seeing the segment the evening news ran on the death behind the bookshop, right?" Lou asked.

"Yeah, although it's no wonder they haven't gotten a single lead. The sketch they put up looked nothing like the guy, if you ask me," Willow grumbled.

"They don't have any leads?" Lou's heart sank.

Kathleen had gotten her hopes up, making it sound like Easton solved crimes in his sleep. A quick end to this case was the only thing she could think to ease the suspicion surrounding the store.

"I mean, I don't know for sure, but Easton's been grumpier than usual today. OC didn't even eat the best carrot in his garden, and he acted like he'd ransacked his entire house." Willow paused, and Lou could picture her rolling her eyes toward Easton's home.

Lou tapped her fingers over the keys of the register computer but didn't put enough pressure to press down on any of them. The motion helped her think. Usually, she was pondering how best to word a critique about a manuscript, though, not thinking of ways to solve a murder.

"I mean, the man had to be involved in the book business somehow, don't you think?" Lou asked.

"Why do you?" Willow asked back.

"He mentioned that Kurt Vonnegut short story, for one. There was also that page he left behind with all of those literary titles jotted down on the back. He was looking for Kimberly for another, so that's what makes me think he's in the bookstore business." Lou wished she could think of more than three reasons. The gut feeling she had about him wasn't something she wanted to bring up, even to Willow, and the ink on his hand could've come from any old pen.

"Maybe you should help in the search, then," Willow suggested.

"Me?" Lou almost dropped her phone in surprise.

Once the doubt subsided, Lou thought of what Noah had said earlier about the kitten. *It's a very lucky thing you found this little guy. I don't think he would've made it outside much longer in this weather we're having.* And hadn't she just been thinking about that stranger in Central Park who'd helped her find Ben when he'd had his heart attack? Without her, Lou would've gone hours or days longer before finding out what had happened to her husband.

"It's not like you're getting involved in the murder part of the investigation. Just put that detail-oriented mind of yours to use figuring out the identity of the man in the alley. I'm sure once he has that information, Easton can't mess it up too badly from there." The last part of the sentence was muffled, as if Willow had meant it for someone other than Lou, as if she'd said it in the direction of Easton's home.

Lou tapped her fingers on the keyboard again, loving the clicking sound they made. It wasn't a terrible idea. In fact, considering helping made Lou feel the most in control she had since the man had spun into her shop the other day.

"You might have something there, Willow," Lou said. "You just got one thing wrong."

"What's that?" Willow asked, a grin coating her words.

"If I'm finding out who he was, you're going to help me."

CHAPTER 8

Lou worked in the bookshop during the day that Monday. She got all the books on the shelf entered in her inventory system and was feeling like she was making real progress.

Taking breaks to play with Romeow was a welcome distraction. Sapphy had left his wild-kitten phase behind years ago and had become quite the lazy cat, sleeping most of the day. It was kind of fun for Lou to have a playful kitten around again.

Once Romeow had gotten some good sleep and food in him, his energy returned. He zoomed around the bookstore as Lou cleaned.

Willow picked Lou up as soon as she finished teaching for the day. She'd used some of her planning time to make a list of the local bookstores and book-related businesses in Lakeside County. While it was possible that the mystery man in the alley was from the larger city of Seattle to the south, the women figured starting in the neighboring towns first made the most sense.

"Lakeside County is made up of three cities and two towns. Button is one of the towns. Brine is the other." Willow rolled her eyes. "Being the smallest is the only thing we have in common with Brine," Willow said, hinting at a long-seeded rivalry with the town to the east. "We're cute as a button and they're salty as brine." She chuckled to herself.

"What makes them salty?" Lou asked. Her taxi had driven through Brine on the way in, and while it definitely wasn't as cutesy as her new home, she'd thought it seemed like fun.

"They're named after pickle juice, for one." Willow barked out a laugh. "They try way too hard. If their intention is to be cute, it turns out weird. What's more, a pickle factory employs most of their town."

Lou pressed her lips together, realizing this was something she shouldn't push. It sounded like the different boroughs of New York. Brooklyn people thought Manhattanites were snobs, and Manhattanites rolled their eyes at Brooklyn's trendiness.

"Okay, so Button and Brine. What else?" Lou stared out the window.

"Then there's Silver Lake. It's the second most populated city and really nice. Too big for my taste, but I know a few teachers who live there." Willow paused at a stop sign and then proceeded. "After that, you have Tinsdale and Kirk. Tinsdale is kind of sad. It used to be home to a major metal manufacturing plant, but it shut down, and the city has become a skeleton of itself ever since. People either moved or got jobs in the surrounding cities. Kirk is the biggest. That's where the Lowe's, Trader Joe's, and Costco are." Willow laughed, giving away where she usually shopped when she visited that city.

"And where are we heading?" Lou asked as they passed by a sign that read *Thanks for visiting Button. Until your next visit.*

"Tinsdale doesn't have much of anything, let alone a bookstore. I figured we could start with Silver Lake today. There's a weird used bookstore in Brine, so we could stop there on the way back if we strike out. Kirk has mostly big box bookstores like Barnes and Noble."

Willow had cut out the police sketch of the mystery man in the alley from the local paper and placed it between them in the center console of her car. Lou grabbed a pen from her purse and drew black-rimmed glasses on the man. She outlined a black fedora and drew that on the picture as well. While he hadn't been wearing a hat or glasses, there had been the crease in his hair and indents on either side of the bridge of his nose. Satisfied that this looked a lot more like the man she'd met, she refolded the clipping and stuck it in her purse.

Willow hadn't been exaggerating. Silver Lake was a really nice place. Whereas Button had a few small lakes—they were more like ponds, really, the city of Silver Lake surrounded one expansive, shimmering body of water with many homes on its waterfront. The business sector of town held smaller establishments that reminded Lou of the shops in Button.

They pulled up in front of a cute brick building with a sign on the window that read *Silver Lake Books*.

"The shop name painted on the glass like that looks really nice," Lou said, thinking about the somewhat dingy Button Books sign hanging over the door. She made a mental note to look into what it would cost to have an artist do that for her business.

"It does," Willow said, putting the car in park.

They climbed out and Lou readied the police sketch as they entered the bookshop. She took more mental notes as they entered, loving a swiveling bookmark display that was almost as tall as she was and a table full of books that held a sign that read *I can't remember the title, but the cover was green.* It was an adorable shop, and seeing how Willow and Lou had to crowd inside with the ten other people already shopping, it was popular as well.

Catching movement behind the checkout counter, Lou elbowed Willow. They walked over and stood on the other side, waiting for the shopkeeper to stand up from where he was crouched. Lou got the sketch ready, laying it out on the counter.

Willow cleared her throat. "Excuse us, but you wouldn't recognize this—?"

But the last word stuck as the man behind the counter stood. He wore slacks, a crisp cotton button-up shirt, black-rimmed glasses, and a gray fedora. Although there were vast differences between him and the man in the alley, the poor police sketch they had set in front of them looked exactly like this man.

He frowned, glancing from the drawing up at their reddening faces. "What is this?" he asked, annoyance edging his tone.

Lou tried to get her thoughts to stop scrambling and line up at least one coherent sentence so she could explain why they were here. Willow stood stock still and just as silent next to her.

The man's frown lines deepened as he returned his focus to the sketch. "That's the police sketch of the man who died one town over. I recognize it." He pointed at the newspaper clipping accusingly. "But you've added a hat and glasses to make it look like me. Is this some kind of joke?"

"No, it's …" Willow rocked back on her heels. "So you don't know this man?"

"You mean, me? Of course I know *me.*" His voice rose in

volume, and a few of the other customers craned their necks to see what was happening.

As uncomfortable as the situation was, Lou had too many questions to retreat. First, how did this man look so similar to the one who died in her alley? Were they brothers? It didn't seem to be the case. Though they dressed the same, their facial features were very different. This man had a larger nose and completely different shaped eyes. The fact that he resembled the sketch spoke more about how wrong the artist's rendition was.

"I know it's weird, and it looks a lot like you," Lou said calmly, trying to reason with the man, "but it's not you. The police sketch is a little off. That's why no one is coming forward. Do you know of anyone else in the book business locally who dresses like this ... like you?" she asked.

The shopkeeper narrowed his eyes as some of the anger left his face. But he shook his head all the same. "No. I don't know of any other booksellers who look like this," he said through gritted teeth.

Lou got the impression that he enjoyed thinking he was one of a kind. Her insinuation that there could be more people who not only dressed like him but also held the same job was an affront to his hard-fought individualism.

"What about customers?" Willow asked a lot less calmly. Her patience with this man was running thin. "Maybe there aren't any other booksellers, but have you seen anyone else who has anything to do with buying books in the area that looks like this?"

"No." The word was as final as his expression.

Lou took the sketch from the counter. "We're sorry to waste your time." She shoved the clipping back in her purse and grabbed Willow's arm, yanking her toward the front door.

She hadn't realized how hot it had become in there until she stepped out into the crisp winter air. They walked to the car, but neither of them got inside right away. Glancing at each other over the roof, they broke into laughter.

"That was the most awkward thing I've encountered in a while, and that's saying something, given that I teach high schoolers." Willow wrinkled her nose.

The relief of getting out of that situation washed over Lou. "He must've thought we were creeps."

Trailing a finger under her eyes to wipe away happy tears, Willow climbed into the car. "We kinda were. It definitely looked like we changed the sketch to look like him," she said as Lou slid into the passenger seat. Willow sat back and put her hands on the steering wheel. "Okay, lesson for the next place. Wait until we see the person first *before* showing the sketch."

Lou agreed, and they drove to a storefront that held a sign in the window that announced *Books Sold Here*, but no business name that they could see.

This shop smelled mustier than the last one. Whereas Silver Lake Books sold new books, this one obviously specialized in used. It was interesting to Lou how much that changed the smell of the space. The glossy, newly printed versions had a heartier, more robust scent. But there was something wonderful about the muted smell as books aged. It felt more authentic, like they'd stopped trying so hard to be impressive and settled into who they really were.

The man behind the counter wore a blue baseball cap and a threadbare, hooded sweatshirt. Lou and Willow shared a quick nod before approaching him. He looked nothing like the sketch. It wasn't like Lou had really thought such a coincidence would happen again, but it was a relief all the same.

"How can I help you two?" The man peeled his attention away from the computer screen in front of him.

"Hi, we're wondering if you know this man?" Lou presented the sketch, laying it flat on the counter facing the shop owner.

He squinted at it, then removed his baseball cap. Using the same hand that held the hat, he scratched at his scalp, then set the cap back on his head. "I'm sorry. He doesn't look familiar to me. Is he missing?"

"Sort of," Willow said. "We have a hunch that he was involved with book sales in the area, and we're just checking around to all the local stores."

The man exhaled. "Yeah, no one I know." He squinted. "Though ... now that you mention book sales, this does kind of resemble Rupert over at Silver Lake Books. Have you checked there?"

Willow bit back a snort.

"We have," Lou jumped in. "It's not him. Thank you for your time." She collected the sketch and folded it back into her purse.

"There's the library," Willow suggested as they walked back to her car, checking her watch. "They close in twenty minutes, as do most of these local stores."

That was one thing Lou knew would take time to get used to. In the city, things were almost always open. If you needed something in the middle of the night, there was a place to find it. Out here, you could hardly find a shop that stayed open past five. She supposed she would become one of those businesses whenever she was able to open her doors, though, so she couldn't complain too much.

Willow drove them to the library, but the woman behind

the circulation desk didn't recognize the man in the sketch either.

"I'd say it's a safe bet this guy wasn't from Silver Lake." Willow kicked at a rock as they exited the library.

But Lou wasn't right behind her like Willow thought. Something on the community board in the entryway to the library had caught Lou's eye. It was a flyer for a Lakeside County book swap.

"This might be another place we could ask around about our mystery man." Lou pointed to the bright pink paper pinned to the corkboard.

"Saturday at nine." Willow dipped her head. "We could do that."

Lou got out her phone and snapped a picture of the information. "And if we have to go empty handed with information, like today, at least we could pick up some books so it's not a total waste." She led the way back to Willow's car.

"Today *does* feel like a bit of a waste, doesn't it?" Willow climbed in and buckled her seat belt.

Lou hated to admit it, but defeat was definitely the primary emotion she was experiencing after hours of searching.

"You know what makes most bad days better?" Willow asked as she pulled up in front of Button Books a short while later. The sun had set, and an icy darkness had settled over Button.

"Snuggling with kittens," Lou said with a big smile. "Do you want to come inside and spend some time with little Romeow?"

Willow laughed. "I was going to say barbecue, but kitten snuggling sounds good too. I can come in for a bit, but we could head over to the Three Bs and grab dinner after that."

Lou unlocked the front door of the bookstore. "That sounds perf—"

But the sight that met her when she entered was far from perfect. The mess stopped her in her tracks, and Willow plowed into the back of Lou, not seeing she'd stopped.

"Ooohhff." Willow's long limbs windmilled as she fought to keep her balance. "What is ...? Oh ..." She stared at the shredded remains of two paperback books sitting in the middle of the bookshop.

In the center of the chaos, an orange kitten slept soundly, his paws tucked under his small, destructive body.

CHAPTER 9

The next day, Lou was working on ordering new stock when there was a knock on the window closest to the register. Romeow woke where he napped on the table next to Sapphy. Lou gritted her teeth. She'd just gotten the kitten to settle and sleep.

An older woman, stooped over as if her back ached, waved at Lou through the window, a handkerchief fluttering in her hand. Her nose was red, and she swiped the handkerchief at it again. She motioned over toward the front door.

Lou frowned. She'd made a clearly worded sign on the door that said she wouldn't be open for a few weeks still. An exhale vented the worst of Lou's frustrations. This woman wasn't the first to ignore Lou's sign that day. A few customers had stopped by wanting to tell Lou how excited they were for her to open, and she couldn't really get mad at that—even if it interrupted her work.

Clicking the lock open, Lou pulled the door toward her, but kept her foot behind it so the woman would see she couldn't invite her inside. "Hello. I'm so sorry, but I'm not open yet. I'll post the reopening date on the door here once I know for sure when that'll be."

The woman waved her handkerchief at Lou. "Oh, I'm not here for books," she said in a way that made Lou wonder if she should take offense.

It was then that Lou spotted three cat crates sitting in the alcove leading into the front entrance.

"I overheard Kathleen over at the veterinary clinic mention you took in that little kitten you found on the side of the road." She pointed to Romeow through the window as if Lou might've forgotten about him. Then the woman's face peeled into a desperate smile. "Well, you see ..." She blew her nose again. "My big sister, Agatha, just passed away."

"I'm so sorry to hear that," Lou said, leaning into the door.

"Yes, it's very sad." The woman rushed through the statement, sounding more inconvenienced than grieving. "The thing is, she left her three cats to me."

"That's very nice." Lou knew her words were more hopeful than anything else, because very nice or not, three cat crates sat in front of her bookshop, which didn't bode well for the sister's last will and testament.

"It would've been," the older woman scoffed. "If I wasn't *severely* allergic." She spat out the word *severely* as if the intensity aided in Lou believing it to be true.

Lou's eyebrows climbed higher on her forehead. She stood there silently, waiting.

"Anyway ..." The woman looked up through her mascara clumped lashes, as if she were trying to appear pitiful. "If you're already fostering one cat, I don't see why you couldn't add a couple more." She wafted the handkerchief toward Lou again as if the motion erased the fact that she'd used the word *couple* instead of *few*.

"Oh," Lou sputtered out the word in surprise even though she felt strongly she should've seen the request coming.

"To foster, of course," the older woman added. "Just until they're adopted."

"Barb can't take them?" Lou asked, using the same name Noah had mentioned when he'd brought up fostering.

"Noah says she's full up, apparently." She rolled her eyes as if she didn't believe that for a second.

Pulling in a deep breath, Lou tried to buy herself some time to think.

"They're very sweet. Two boys and a girl. Or was it two girls and a boy?" The woman tapped her fingers against her lips. "I'm sure they had names, but I can't, for the life of me, remember them. I've just been calling them Orangey, Whitey, and Grayie."

Grayie? Lou's mouth pulled into an unimpressed line. For some reason, that uninspired name was the deciding factor for Lou. She had a few weeks until she could open, anyway. If this helped get this woman off Noah's back, she could do that.

"Okay, I can take them." She opened the door.

The woman pressed her hands together in thanks. "You're amazing. I'm Jeanine, by the way. So lovely to meet you. I have food and litter for them too." She pointed to a bag behind her.

Lou waved her inside. "Bring it all in. The more the merrier."

Jeanine stuck around for all of three seconds after setting down the final cat crate and handing over the bag of food and litter. Lou had to laugh and shake her head as she knelt by the crates and peeked inside. Sapphy and Romeow climbed down from the table to investigate as Lou opened up the crates. She watched the proceedings warily, knowing Romeow and

Sapphy getting along right away wasn't the norm. She prepared for hissing.

A beautiful gray tabby stuck a tentative paw out first. It blinked gorgeous blue eyes at her, much lighter than Sapphy's striking jewel-toned ones. The gray tabby—Grayie, she guessed—stretched and walked over to her, rubbing up against her hand.

"Hi, sweetheart," Lou cooed. "Welcome to your new temporary home."

Grayie left to investigate Sapph and Romeow, but it seemed to go well because the new cat moved on to smelling the bookshelves next. A calico darted out of the next crate, not even giving Lou a hello. It automatically hid under the table, wide, green eyes staring back at her. Romeow pounced behind it, ready to play, but the older cat growled at him and he backed away.

"I'm not sure if you're Orangey or Whitey since you have both colors in your coat." Lou wrinkled her nose. She peered inside the final crate to find an adult version of Romeow inside, pressed against the back of the crate. "Ah, so you're Orangey and you must be Whitey," she addressed the calico who had slunk underneath a different chair under the table.

Lou held her hand forward, careful not to enter the crate and cause the cat to feel cornered or threatened. Luckily, Jeanine was right about the cats being sweet. The orange cat meowed and came forward to meet Lou's outstretched hand.

And then they all jumped when someone knocked on the front window. Four out of the five cats rocketed into the air and then scattered. Sapphy, who was the only one who hadn't heard the knock, crouched low as he studied the other cats' reactions and wondered if he should run.

Lou pulled him into her arms and stood. Noah stood at

the door. His face contorted into a grimace, and his eyes darted around the room as he watched the cats run. There was also a tightness to his posture that spoke of frustration. For someone who'd had such an easy, calming manner the last couple of times she'd seen him, the change in his demeanor surprised Lou. She hoped she hadn't made him mad.

Opening the door, she let him inside.

"I was walking by when I noticed you seemed to have three new residents." Noah pinched the bridge of his nose.

Lou craned her neck to see if any of them were venturing out from their temporary hiding places. "Yeah, a lady named—"

"Jeanine just dropped them off?" Noah guessed, running a hand through his hair. His dark eyes softened as they met hers. "Look, Lou, you didn't have to do this. She was at the clinic earlier and tried to get us to take them. Kathleen worried Jeanine had overheard her telling someone else about how you'd taken in that kitten …" He trailed off, frustration coating his words. He didn't need to finish, though. It was obvious what had happened.

Lou smiled. "It's okay, really. I'm a New Yorker, remember? I can stand up for myself. I took them because I wanted to. I have several more weeks before I'll be able to open anyway, so what's a few more cute cats hanging around?" She placed a hand on his arm but pulled it away to gesture at the group of cats congregating on the floor. "See? They're getting along."

Even the shy calico had come out from under the table and was sniffing at Romeow.

Noah stuffed his hands in his pockets. "Okay, if you're sure. What are you going to do if we can't find homes for them before you open?"

Lou stroked Sapphy's soft head and chewed on the inside of her lip for a moment. "I have room up in my apartment."

"Or you could run a cat café only in bookshop form," Noah joked.

Lou beamed. "I visited one of those when I was in Japan a couple years back for a conference." She tilted her head. "You know, now that you mention it, that's not such a bad idea. What more could people ask for than a bookshop full of cats they could adopt if they form a connection?"

Noah laughed. "True. It could work."

At that moment, Romeow jumped up onto a bookshelf and stared menacingly at a paperback. "Oh, no you don't." Lou set Sapphy down on the table and grabbed Romeow instead. "It'll work if this one doesn't rip up any more books." She scowled down at the kitten, but her anger fell away as he purred happily.

Noah reached forward to scratch the kitten's back. "I can at least work on getting this one adopted quickly, then," he said. "Kittens are usually the easiest to find homes for. I'll reach out to a few more people today."

"Thanks. He'll be perfect for someone who hates to read." She chuckled. As much of a tiny terror as Sapphire had been— and their furniture had paid the price—he'd never hurt a book in his life.

"At least you know these three are in great health." Noah knelt to scoop up the friendly gray cat. "I just did exams on them all today."

"You don't remember what Agatha called them, do you?" Lou asked. "Jeanine was calling them Grayie, Whitey, and Orangey." Lou wrinkled her nose and pointed to each cat as she recited its name.

Noah's shoulders shook as he chuckled. "I'm afraid her

sister wasn't any more creative. That was Tails. That was Whiskers." Noah pointed to the orange cat. "And this is Fluffy," he said, bouncing the gray cat in his arms.

Lou screwed up her lips. "Oh, come on. The naming of cats is a difficult matter."

"Is it?" Noah asked with a smile.

"You haven't read that poem by T. S. Eliot?" Lou asked.

Noah squinted one eye. "Can't say I have. We didn't study poetry much in veterinary school."

Smiling, Lou said, "Understandable. Basically, Eliot says each cat has three names. Their everyday name, their fancy name, and the name that only they know. Names like Fluffy or Grayie won't get these kids adopted. A strong name like Romeow, though, that's going to catch someone's eye." She booped the kitten's little pink nose affectionately.

"Romeow." Noah nodded, impressed. "Definitely fitting. And who doesn't love a literary reference in a bookshop?"

"Right?" Lou sucked in a breath. "That's it. We need to come up with literary names for all of you." She folded her arms. "I think I was born to do this."

"Well, you hit a home run with the first one." Noah set down the gray cat.

"Technically, that was all Willow. But I'll figure it out." She set the kitten down and patted the fur off her sweater. "Thank you for the idea."

Noah grinned, that dimple deepening. He looked like he was back to his laid-back self, and Lou was glad that she'd been able to calm his worries.

Glancing down at the large bag of supplies, Noah said, "Well, the least I can do is help you set up their litter boxes and find places for their food dishes."

Lou accepted his help and showed him the office. "This is

going to be a lot of litter. I'm thinking the back room is going to have to be the place."

Noah got to work, but before he could disappear around the corner into the office, she called out, "Oh, wait." He paused. "Girls or boys? Jeanine couldn't remember that either. It'll help with their names."

"Girl." Noah pointed at Grayie. "Girl." He pointed at Whitey next. "And boy." He finished with Orangey. "All fixed. Don't worry."

"Perfect," Lou said with a nod. While he worked on the litter boxes in the back, she set up food dishes and poured them each a small amount.

When the gray cat came over and rubbed against her leg before moving to eat, Lou said, "Okay, little girl. Let me look at you."

She picked up the cat and inspected her. She was beautiful, but one of her most prominent features was that her canine teeth kind of stuck out below her lip, giving her a vampiric quality. Sticking with the literary theme, Lou thought about books with vampires.

"What about the name Anne Mice, for you? After the writer Anne Rice. She wrote about vampires," Lou explained.

The cat purred in response. Or maybe it was merely happy about the food. Lou chose to believe it was an endorsement for her new name. In fact, the cat almost seemed to hold herself differently now that she had a more respectable name.

A new name.

Lou thought about the nagging worry she'd had since the bad press surrounding Button Books. Maybe what she needed was a new name for the shop. If she was going to have to get updated signs made anyway, it might be nice to have a fresh start.

CHAPTER 10

That Saturday morning, Willow and Lou stopped by the Bean and Button to grab coffees before driving out to Silver Lake for the book swap.

"So how's cat-a-palooza going?" Willow asked with a chuckle.

Lou squinted one eye. "Overall, fine. It's actually just my little Romeow creating all the trouble. The other three are doing great. Sapph seems unaffected by all of it." She shrugged.

"And did you come up with the other names?" Willow stepped forward as the coffee line moved.

"I did." Lou's expression brightened. "The gray is Anne Mice."

Willow nodded, having heard that one already.

"The little orange-and-white calico is going to be Catnip Everdeen." Lou couldn't help the grin that peeled across her face.

"Like Katniss from *The Hunger Games*. Because she's good at fighting?" Willow asked, giving Lou a sidelong glance.

Lou held up a finger. "Actually, it's because she's always aware, watching her back, and staying on the alert."

Willow laughed. "Okay. And the orange one?"

"I settled on Purrt Vonnegut. In honor of our mystery man and his muttered reference to Kurt Vonnegut's *Harrison Bergeron*."

"I like it." They stepped up to the counter and ordered. When they'd paid and waited for their order, Willow asked, "And you're really into this whole idea of running a cat adoption bookshop?"

"I am." The idea had only cemented itself in her brain and heart as the week had progressed. "I'm thinking of making them little profile sheets to hang in the windows or at the checkout counter. I'll add a picture, their name, and some of their personality traits. And I worked out an adoption process that Noah said he'd take care of. The fee is pretty minimal, but Noah insisted I use it to purchase items for the fostered cats."

"Sounds like you've got it figured out." Willow's shoulders dropped in relief.

Lou could tell she'd been a little apprehensive about the plan at first. Lou had planned on having Sapphy with her in the bookshop each day, but there was a considerable difference between one deaf cat who slept all day to a handful of other felines roaming about the place.

"You should see me walking down the stairs in the morning." Lou laughed. "It's like a tiny herd following me."

"They've been coming upstairs at night?" Willow cocked an eyebrow.

Lou nodded. "I can't trust Romeow down there alone. And Sapphy comes with me, of course. Anne Mice and Purrt Vonnegut just followed us up. The only one who stayed downstairs all night was Catnip Everdeen. But I watched her on the interior camera, and she seems to love the alone time. She's usually hiding under things, but when she was alone, she just plopped in the middle of the floor and stretched out."

Their coffees were ready, and they walked outside toward where Willow had parked. Lou held open the coffee shop door for Easton as he jogged toward them. He waved in thanks, but just as he grabbed the door, his phone rang. He took the call, stepping back outside. Lou overheard him say, "Tinsdale? Okay. Out by the truck stop? Gotcha. I'm on my way." Then he turned on his heel and ran back to his car without a coffee.

"Must've been an emergency." Willow whistled. "Easton's even more of a grouch if he doesn't get his coffee."

Lou hid a grin as they climbed into the car and headed for Silver Lake. Her friend certainly seemed to know a lot about a man she purported to hate.

The book swap was taking place in the community center building, which seemed to be larger than Button High School. They entered the warm building, glad to get out of the freezing temperatures. Inside, there were tables and booths set up in rows from one end of the large space to the other. Some people had books laid out on tables; others had set up bookshelves, and some had even procured old library carts on which to display their books.

Along with the warmth of the space, a different form of coziness wrapped itself around Lou as they walked forward. A room full of books and people who loved books were always welcome, in Lou's mind. The crinkle of paper in her purse reminded her they were there to inquire about the mystery man in her alley, so this wasn't a personal trip. They had work to do.

"Quick pass first?" Willow asked.

Lou agreed, and they snaked through the aisles, mapping out what they noticed and who they might want to talk to.

While there were mostly individuals there selling off books, there were also quite a few local businesses. Those delineated themselves from the individuals by hanging banners next to their spaces or off the front of their tables, listing their business names.

They saw a woman selling her now-grown children's complete sets of the Nancy Drew and Hardy Boys mysteries. Lou would've loved to look, but that booth was crowded, and she predicted that would be a competitive group of buyers. A man had inherited a storage pod full of his grandfather's old books and was selling them off because he only enjoyed reading Stephen King and nothing else. The baseball cap guy had a booth in the corner, and they spotted Silver Lake Books' owner wandering around the stalls, shopping. Willow and Lou skirted past him, hoping he wouldn't recognize them from earlier that week.

As they concluded their first round, Lou and Willow stopped at the entrance again to decide on a plan.

"I think to divide and conquer is our best course of action," Willow said.

"Agreed. Do you think it's worth checking into the Silver Lake Books' guy again since he's here?" Lou asked. "What did that used-book guy call him? Rupert? There might be more to him looking so similar to the mystery man."

Willow's eyebrows rose. "True. Yeah, I think we should investigate further, but it'll be tricky. He might remember us."

"Maybe not if we're apart." Lou glanced up at her taller-than-average friend. "And I think it should be me, since he's more likely to remember you."

"For sure." Willow patted her messenger bag, showing Lou she had her own copy of the police sketch.

They'd found extra copies and cut out three more. Lou had added the hat and glasses to the second copy, so they each had one original and one with the added accessories.

"Meet back here in half an hour," Willow suggested.

Lou saluted her friend, and they headed off in opposite directions. She started with the first stall she came upon, asking the man standing behind the table if he recognized the person in the sketched picture. He didn't, and neither did the next four sellers. Lou even asked a few of the shoppers, none of whom seemed to know the man. The sixth seller she asked, frowned and then peered across the aisle to where Rupert was reading the back cover of a book. His hand rose as he pointed.

"Not him. I know he looks similar, but this man would've been wearing a suit," Lou explained quickly. Relief washed over her as his hand dropped back down to his side.

"Nah." He scratched at his cheek. "Other than that guy, I haven't seen anyone like that."

Lou wrinkled her nose in frustration. No wonder Easton wasn't getting anywhere with the mystery man's identity. Maybe she'd been wrong about the book connection. What if he wasn't connected to the book business at all? Or he might not have been from Lakeside County.

The next four booksellers she asked glanced over at Rupert. Lou took it as her sign to go investigate him further. She sidled over to the crowded stall he was shopping at and wished she had a pair of sunglasses with her, or even a hat. Remembering that her hair had been pulled up into a bun the other day, Lou let it down, combing her fingers through her dark brown waves in hopes it would look different enough. She peeked through her curtain of hair as she approached Rupert, hiding the sketch in her bag, since it would only help to remind him who she was.

This seller had brought portable shelves that were about six feet tall. Lou ducked behind one and watched as Rupert picked up a used copy of *Dune* to inspect. She wracked her brain for something to ask him that might lead her toward information about the mystery man in her alley.

Before Lou could decide on anything, a conversation behind her caught her attention.

"Weird that Frederick doesn't have a display. I thought for sure he'd be here," an older woman said in a shrill, self-important voice.

Lou checked over her shoulder to see the woman talking to the baseball hat guy from the used bookstore. He shrugged, snatching his cap off his head, scratching, and then placing it back on in a practiced movement he'd exhibited when Lou and Willow had visited.

"I thought so too. Can't say I'm sad to see him gone, though." Baseball Cap Guy's expression darkened. "Less competition."

A man these two book people knew was missing? And it sounded like he was a fellow bookseller. This could very well be her mystery man. Intrigue spiked inside Lou, and she followed them as they walked.

The older woman laughed. "That's for sure. Though we're probably getting excited over nothing. Freddie's most likely on some secret book-collecting mission, snatching up all the treasures before we have a chance at them."

Baseball Cap Guy snorted. "You're one to talk, but yeah, Frederick was the worst at that."

Ignoring his cut at her, the older woman said, "Speaking of stealing what isn't yours, I heard you convinced Mrs. Martin to sell you that copy of *The Hobbit* I just sold her for half the price."

The baseball hat came off again. His fingers raked through his hair, and the hat went back again. "Not me. Must've been Frederick."

They continued walking, their voices growing fainter as they left.

Lou's heart hammered in her chest. She had seen an ornate copy of *The Hobbit* on his desk when she and Willow had visited his shop on Monday, which meant that he'd likely just lied to that woman. Many people were liars, so that wasn't a revelation. What had her mind racing with questions was the thing he'd done just before he lied. He took off his baseball hat, scratched his head, and put the cap back on as if it were a nervous tick. He'd also performed the same motion before he'd said he didn't know where this Frederick person was and when he'd told Lou and Willow that he didn't recognize the man in the sketch.

Did the man have a tell? And, more importantly, had he lied about knowing the man in the drawing?

Lou contemplated her options. If he'd lied to her once, who was to say he wouldn't do it again. Maybe she'd have more luck with the woman. Her eyes followed the older woman as she and Baseball Cap Guy went their separate ways. Lou walked behind, closing the distance between her and the woman.

Stopping behind a booth with a sign that said *Used Books Sold Here*, the woman plucked a *Be right back* sign off the table and removed the tablecloth she'd draped over it in her absence. She fluffed her short, white hair and then started as she turned around to see Lou standing there.

"Oh dear. You just about gave an old woman a heart

attack." She placed a hand on her chest and fanned her face with the other.

"I'm so sorry." Lou stepped forward. "I'm looking for anyone who might know the identity of this man." She pulled out the original police sketch and showed it to the woman, having been burned too many times by Rupert's presence at the swap to use the other version.

The older woman backed away and snatched the sketch from Lou's hand, holding it at arm's length, proving she was farsighted. "I've never seen him."

Hoping she wouldn't regret it, Lou swapped out the sketch with the one she'd drawn on. "How about now?"

The woman's eyes lit up. She held the doctored sketch out at arm's length again, and Lou waited for her gaze to flick over to Rupert. But it didn't. Instead, the woman turned her attention back to Lou and said, "Yes, I know him."

Lou glanced over her shoulder. "Not him?" She jerked her head toward the owner of Silver Lake Books.

The older woman shook her head. "Although, now that you mention it, they do look rather alike. But no, this is obviously Frederick. He's a rare-books dealer in the county."

So it had been the Frederick they'd been discussing! Joy filled Lou as she finally put a name to the face of the poor man in her alley.

"What's his last name?" Lou asked.

"Alvarado. He lives in Tinsdale," the woman said.

"And what is the name of the man who's wearing the baseball cap over there?" Lou asked, trying to sound curious instead of desperate for information.

"That's Lance. Lance Swatek." The woman seemed to cue in to the fact that Lou had now asked about two bookdealers, because she leaned closer and said, "There's nothing I could help you find, is there?"

Lou shuffled backward. "No, thank you."

The woman's smiling expression turned stony, and she waved a dismissive hand toward Lou as a customer came over and she turned her attention to them.

Lou didn't mind. She had the information she needed. Scanning the crowd for her best friend, she spotted Willow standing near the Nancy Drew collection. Lou raced over, hooking her arm through Willow's and pulling her off to the side.

"I know who he is," she whispered excitedly.

Willow's eyes grew wide. "Oh good. Because I got nothing."

"His name is Frederick Alvarado, and he's a rare bookseller from Tinsdale." Lou searched the crowd for Baseball Cap Guy. "And, that's not all." She surreptitiously gestured to the man whom they'd talked to on Monday. "I think he lied to us when he said he didn't recognize him."

CHAPTER II

The noise of the book swap fell away as Willow grabbed at Lou's arm and pulled her down the nearest hallway toward the exit.

"This is huge," Willow said. "You figured out who the mystery man was. We need to let Easton know right away."

Lou knew Willow was right. They should tell Easton right away, not stay to shop for books like Lou kind of wanted to —*what was another thirty minutes? Maybe the difference between solving this case or not,* she scolded herself.

With one last longing glance over her shoulder at the book swap, she allowed Willow to guide her away from the books.

There were more important matters at hand. They drove quickly back to Button and pulled into the police station just under half an hour later. Willow and Lou rushed inside.

"Hey Harold," Willow addressed the older officer behind the front desk. "I need to speak with Easton right now. It's urgent."

Harold cocked an eyebrow at her as if he doubted it was, but picked up the phone anyway. He punched in four numbers, then waited. "Hey, you have a minute to come up front?" Harold listened. "Yeah, it's your neighbor," Harold said, his tone flat with disinterest. "Says it's important."

Willow's jaw clenched tight, but she breathed deeply and seemed to let her anger go.

"He'll be right up." Harold smiled in a way that seemed more like a sneer.

Lou pulled Willow away from the front desk so she wouldn't take the confrontation any further. She didn't want her friend to get in trouble for verbally assaulting a member of law enforcement.

Luckily, Easton strode into the room just a few moments later. His eyes flicked from Willow to Lou, then back to Willow.

"What's up?" he asked, his forehead creasing as he stopped in front of them.

"We know the identity of the man in the alley," Willow blurted.

Lou waited for Easton's expression to light up with the news, just as hers had when she'd learned of Frederick's identity.

It didn't.

Instead, Easton ran a tired hand over his face. "Yeah, so do we." He yawned, possibly because he'd never gotten his usual morning coffee.

"What?" Willow glanced at Lou.

"We found out about an hour ago. His name was Frederick Alvarado," Easton said easily as if he'd known all along.

Lou and Willow nodded dejectedly, all the excitement officially knocked out of their news.

"We found his brother's body and when we went to notify

him, and couldn't locate him, realized he fit the profile of our John Doe from Lou's alley," Easton explained.

"Do you think the brother killed Frederick and then killed himself?" Lou asked through a cringe.

Easton's posture tensed. "No, his brother had been dead a couple of days prior to Frederick's death. He was the victim of a hit and run with a semi truck last week, but we didn't find his body until today."

Lou's interest piqued at that information, remembering how Easton had mentioned the truck stop on the phone earlier that morning. That must've been the call he'd taken, the one that had taken precedence over his coffee.

"Well, since it couldn't have been his brother, I'd look into a Lance Swatek," Lou said, "as a person of interest for Frederick's murder," she further clarified. "I'm pretty sure he lied to us about knowing him, and I overheard him talking about how he was glad Frederick was gone today at a book swap. It sounded like they were in competition."

Easton flipped open a notepad and wrote down the name. "Got it. Thanks, Lou."

The women turned to leave as the detective headed back to his office. Once the police station door swung closed behind them, Willow scoffed, "Did you notice how he only thanked you?" She wrestled her keys from her purse. "That man is incorrigible."

"Yeah, he definitely goes out of his way to make you feel less important. Kind of how OC goes out of his way to eat Easton's vegetables." Lou playfully ran her shoulder into Willow's.

Willow's frown turned into a reluctant smile. "At least my horse is getting the better of him."

H<small>UNGRY AFTER THEIR</small> morning of investigating, the two women went out for a pleasant lunch, and Willow dropped Lou off at her place a couple of hours later.

Lou released Romeow from his prison upstairs. Really, he had the whole upstairs apartment to roam around while she was gone, but from the way he yowled and clawed at the door, one would think he was being kept in a tiny cage. She hadn't even left him alone. Sapphy had been asleep on the bed up there too. But the angry kitten glare he gave her as he escaped from the apartment made Lou feel akin to an evil stepmother from a fairy tale, hiding a prince up in a tower against his wishes.

After she fed the cats, Lou sat at the table with her list of tasks in front of her. She'd checked off all the cleaning, had entered the current books into the inventory system, had new books on the way, and had even come up with a few possibilities for alternative names for the shop. She wanted something that spoke to the cat adoption part of the store as well as the books. Her favorite by far was Whiskers and Words.

The idea of giving the shop a whole new identity felt right, and Lou sat there daydreaming about a new logo and how else she might rebrand the shop.

She started a list of things she would need to order. First, she needed to talk to an artist about a logo. Then she could order custom bookmarks, some mugs, and even cat toys with the name of the shop sewn on to them.

Hours went by as she jotted down her notes, searched online, and worked to make this new part of her dream a reality. She messaged three different graphic design artists for quotes and had narrowed the merchandise vendors down to her favorite two. If she hadn't been sitting right next to the front window, she wouldn't have even realized the sun had set until her stomach grumbled.

Appraising the bookshop, Lou grinned. It was quite the scene. Sapphy was asleep on a stack of books on one shelf, while Anne Mice rolled onto her back contentedly on another. Purrt Vonnegut was on the shelf above Sapph, swatting playfully at a book that was tottering, about to fall toward Sapphy. Romeow was curled up in her lap, and Catnip Everdeen had crawled out from her hiding spot and was lying with her back pressed up to the nearest bookshelf, purring away as she napped.

A bookshop full of cats. It was a delightful sight.

Lou added the cat bio sheets to her to-do list and then scooped up Romeow. She had some leftovers from lunch and needed a little fuel if she was going to keep knocking items off her list. But before she could leave the table, her phone buzzed with a notification.

It was a notification from her security cameras. They'd picked up movement.

At first, Lou thought it had been her to trip the inside camera with her movement. But a check of the time told her she still had an hour until that would've been the case. Her heart raced as she opened the camera and saw a live image of the back alley again. In the black-and-white footage, she saw a figure lurking by her back door. They wore a long coat and a hood pulled up over their head.

The figure paced, stopped in front of the back door, and then paced again.

Anger rose inside Lou. It matched the figure that had stopped by the first day she'd installed the cameras. She took a quick screen shot, texted it to Easton, and then set down Romeow.

Easton responded right away. *On my way.*

Lou relaxed at his message. But as she monitored the video footage, she noticed the figure move away from the door as if they knew the police were coming. Lou's nose twitched, and she regarded the locked right-hand drawer next to her cash register. She'd stashed her stun gun there when she'd first arrived, sure she wouldn't need it any longer now that she wasn't living in a big city.

Racing over, she unlocked the drawer, brought out the stun gun, and raced toward the back alley. Her flashlight was pointed forward, the stun gun primed in her other hand as she pushed open the door.

The figure moved to run, but Lou called out, "Stop right there" in her best, tough New Yorker tone.

The person stopped, but they stayed put with their back to Lou. She gritted her teeth for courage and stepped forward.

"What do you want? Why do you keep coming here?" She kept her voice steady.

The cloaked figure remained silent.

"Answer me. The cops are on the way," Lou threatened.

Instead of answering, the figure let out a low meow.

Lou squinted, trying to see in the darkness.

"Did you just ... meow?" she asked.

Turning around, the person stepped into the light. It was a man. He couldn't have been much older than Lou. He wore a black beanie and had pulled the hood of a gray sweatshirt up to cover his head.

He blinked at the brightness of her flashlight, but even after she pointed it down so it wasn't directly in his eyes, his face remained in a grimace. "I'm sorry. I-I didn't know where else to go."

Lou tried to piece together what was happening when a light flashed behind her.

"Lou?" Easton's voice bounced down the alley toward them.

"Over here," she called, keeping her attention on the man in front of her.

Footsteps rang behind her and before she knew it, Easton stood next to her, holding his flashlight down just like she was.

"Danny?" Easton asked, ducking his head as if he couldn't quite get a good view.

The man pushed back his hoodie, pulling the beanie off at the same time. "Yeah, it's me, East."

"What are you doing creeping around Lou's back door?" Easton's voice held a much lighter tone than it had before, making Lou sure he knew this man well enough to realize he wasn't a threat.

"He meowed," Lou said, pointing toward the man.

"It wasn't me." The man reached into his coat and produced a cat so black, Lou almost couldn't see it in the darkness. "It was Shadow, our cat."

Easton and Lou waited for him to continue.

Danny's eyes were rimmed with dark circles as if he hadn't had a good night's sleep in longer than he could remember. His whole body seemed to sag forward with the weight of fatigue.

"Our daughter doesn't want him anymore. She says he's too mean, and my wife and I hate cleaning the litter box, and he scratched up our entire couch." Danny held the cat away from his body as if it might scratch him if he let it get closer. "I heard the lady who owned the new bookstore was taking in cats no one else wanted, and I was thinking I could just leave him back here." Danny's head had not been held high in the first place, but with that admission, it dropped even lower in shame.

Despite his sad demeanor, Lou felt no sympathy for the man. "You were going to leave him out here during the winter? Why not just come to my front door and ask?" Her tone hadn't changed from the harsh one she'd used when she thought he was dangerous.

"I was too embarrassed. I didn't want people to think we were the kind of people to give back a pet. We've never done this before." Danny winced as if saying the words hurt him.

Easton stepped forward. "You don't have to take this cat, Lou. Danny, you need to go through the proper channels with stuff like this. Leaving the cat here, outside, would've been animal abuse. It's freezing. You have to think clearer. Here, let me take you to see Noah, and we can figure something out."

But Lou's heart hurt for the poor, unwanted cat. She put her stun gun away and stepped forward. "No, I'll take him. Here." She held out her arms for the cat.

Relief washed over Danny's tired features.

"Shadow deserves to be somewhere he's loved," Lou said as she took the cat in her arms.

Danny winced again but nodded.

The cat's claws sank into Lou's arm but not maliciously. The poor thing was terrified and probably freezing cold. She took it inside, but Easton's scolding tones echoed off the frozen walls of the alley behind her.

CHAPTER 12

The following Monday was a pretty big one for Lou. Her first shipment of books came in that morning. The giddiness that enveloped her felt akin to the days during elementary school when book orders would show up. Coming back to class after recess to find a stack of brand new, perfect books on her desk was one of the greater joys of her young life.

Opening the boxes of brand new books definitely measured up. Until the cats got involved. She wasn't even halfway done unpacking the first of four boxes when Romeow started chewing on the corner of the box. Meanwhile, Purrt chased Anne around the box. The Great Catsby—formerly Shadow—kept trying to jump inside the box even though it was still half filled with books.

Sapphire lay on the table, peeking open one blue eye as he observed the madness unfolding. Lou placed a hand on her hip, the other one swiped at her forehead.

"Sapph, have I told you lately that you're my favorite?" She blew a kiss to her cat.

He closed his eye and flicked his tail in response.

"Now, for the rest of you, I need some space. This is an important day for me." All the cats stopped. Well, all except Romeow, who watched her, but continued to chew on the flap of the box as he listened.

Ten minutes later—and four full bowls of cat food to distract them, Lou was finally unloading the box in peace. She'd gone with a mix of new releases and classics in this order, and she was happy with the selection it would offer customers. After entering the new books into the computer, she piled them into genres on the table next to the register and started ferrying them over to the proper shelves.

She'd just put the last stack away when the cats finished with their food distractions and wandered back in.

"Okay, friends. It's all yours." She gestured to the box.

They raced toward it. A good half hour of jumping in the box, surprising each other by vaulting out of the box, chewing on the box, and ripping a flap off the box commenced. Lou was practically in stitches as she monitored them while she opened the second box in peace. She reminded herself to keep a decoy box on hand in the future to make these delivery days go a lot easier.

At one point, The Great Catsby had wandered away from the boxes and tried to scratch at the old love seat in the center of the shop, as Danny had complained he had the propensity to do. Lou had prepared for such an event, and pulled out a spray bottle full of water, spritzing the area next to the cat at the same time she gave him a scolding, "No." The black cat jumped and backed away.

When he tried scratching again on the side of one bookshelf a little while later, Lou was ready again. She repeated the verbal warning with the spray of water. Catsby flinched and ran away even though the water hadn't touched him. Based on his reaction, Lou guessed it wouldn't take many more reminders for him to learn. She also made a note to grab a handful of cat scratchers at the local pet store.

Once she finished emptying all four of the boxes, entered them in the computer, and put the rest away, she gazed out at her shop. It was wild what a difference fuller shelves made. She hadn't even filled them, either, leaving spaces for the cats —particularly Sapphy—to sleep on each shelf, knowing how much he enjoyed the higher vantage point.

It was a decision she regretted almost immediately. She was heading to the bathroom when Romeow, who must've been lurking at the top of a bookshelf, pounced onto her head, claws extended. Lou screamed in surprise, her hands coming up to pry the kitten off her. His green eyes had been alight with self-satisfaction and mischief when she held him in front of her.

"Oh, Romeow," Lou groaned. "What am I going to do with you? I'm getting close to being able to open, and I can't have you attacking customers as they peruse the shelves," Lou scolded the kitten. "You've got a couple of weeks to get your act together, sir." She set down the kitten and sighed as he scampered away, looking like he'd learned nothing.

A red flashing light over by the computer caught her eye.

"What's this?" She wandered over to where the shop phone sat in its cradle. A red number one flashed in the small screen labeled *Messages*. "I didn't even hear it ring," she muttered to herself.

She looked back at the cats, none of whom were paying any attention to her. She knew it was a little silly how much she talked to Sapphy, but somehow talking to cats who could hear didn't make it any better. Checking the phone, she realized why she hadn't heard it ring. Someone had turned the volume all the way down.

"This seems like more of Kimberly's doing," Lou mused with slightly gritted teeth.

She made sure the volume was up loud enough that she could hear it ring next time before playing the message.

The message started out with some heavy breathing. Lou wrinkled her nose, wondering if someone had accidentally dialed the number from their pocket. But then a low, menacing voice said, "I know what you did. I don't know how you put it past me, but believe me, you'll pay for this. I've told everyone I know not to trust you or to shop at Button Books. You can avoid my calls all you want, but you can't avoid me. Eventually, I will find you." The message clicked off.

Lou shivered. *What had Kimberly gotten herself into?* Even though the cryptic message was obviously meant for the shop's former owner, the malice in the man's voice made another tingle squirm down her spine.

As much as Lou wanted to erase the message and be done with it, she knew this might be important for Easton to hear, so she saved it. He could look up the phone number and get the name of whoever had just threatened her—well, threatened Kimberly, but still. Whoever called obviously didn't know Kimberly no longer owned Button Books.

The message made Lou even more sure about the name change and rebranding she was planning for the business.

A metallic clink to her left kicked her out of her thoughts. "Romeow," she stretched his name out like a complaint. The kitten had gotten up on the bookshelves again. Lou jumped up from where she sat at the table and rushed over to him. He was batting at something with his little paw, but Lou realized it wasn't a book. It fell to the floor with a clatter and a metallic ping. Romeow dove after it as if it were a live animal, and he needed to chase it down.

When Lou crouched to investigate, she found a brass dimple key.

She gasped in a lungful of air. A memory of Frederick tapping anxiously on the table with a similar key flashed into her thoughts from that night he'd stopped by. Had the book page been only *one of* the things he left behind? Doubt turned down the corners of her mouth. Was it the same key? It wasn't as if they were rare. But someone had obviously stashed this key in between two books on a shelf just about chest height.

Lou peered back at the table, then toward the back door where he'd fled. He would've passed right by that bookshelf. Had he hidden this key? And from what or whom had he run?

Doubts aside about whether this was the same key, she needed to show Easton.

Tucking Romeow under her arm, she took him upstairs and put him in the apartment. The other cats were still busy with the empty box she'd left behind, so she figured they would be fine. She eyed Catsby, but he gave her such an innocent look in return that she decided to trust him. Grabbing her jacket, Lou headed down the road to the police station.

Outside, the sun was shining deceptively bright for such a frigid day. The air smelled of pine boughs and woodsmoke with just a hint of the sweet waffle-cone scent from the ice cream shop next door. Lou's breath billowed into a frosty cloud as she walked. She shoved her hands into her pockets, her right one gripping the key tight.

The police station was bustling, much busier than it had been during her first visit with Willow. The same older officer sat behind the front desk as last time. She stopped in front of the desk and waited for the man Willow had referred to as

Harold to look up. Not feeling like she was on a first-name basis, she peeked at his badge and read that his last name was Reynolds.

"Whaddaya need?" he asked without looking up.

"Is Detective West available?" she asked.

Reynolds shook his head, still not meeting her eyes. "He's off duty." The man flipped through a few papers on the desk. "For the next couple of days, actually." He shrugged like it made no difference to him. "Already hit his hours for the week, and they're not gonna approve overtime for a case that's basically solved, so he's on his 'weekend.'" Reynolds used air quotes around the last word since it was technically not the regular weekend.

"Oh." Lou gripped the key tighter.

It wasn't as if she didn't trust the other officers, but it was Easton's case. There was also the fact that it might not be the same key as the one Frederick had been holding on to that day. There was a good possibility it was a key that went to something in the bookshop. Maybe she should text Easton instead, or pop over to his place tonight when she was supposed to have dinner with Willow.

Officer Reynolds finally glanced up from his screen. "You're the one he's been dropping everything to go help every few minutes. The new kid in town." He appraised her. "Would you like to leave a message for him?"

Lou's cheeks heated at his comment. Was she calling on Easton too much? He'd told her to let him know if anything happened. Added to her doubt about the key's origin, embarrassment pushed her to hold on to the key.

She pursed her lips. "No. No message. Thanks."

"You okay?" Reynolds studied her closely now. "You look a little freaked out."

"I'm fine." Lou made her best attempt to smile through her unease. "I just got a threatening message on my bookshop voicemail, and it has me a little worried. I'm sure it's nothing."

The hard lines of Reynolds' scowling face softened. He leaned forward. "Listen, word is Kimberly got threatening messages all the time, mostly because she never answered her phone." He snorted.

That made sense, given that she'd down turned the ringer.

"They'll stop calling once they realize she sold the shop and split. Don't you worry about it." Reynolds cocked his head.

"You don't think it's at all connected to the dead man in the alley?" She couldn't help herself. She had to ask.

Reynolds' expression flattened as if he wouldn't have ever considered it. He waved a hand toward her. "Nah, not one bit." He checked right, then left, before leaning closer to her. "To be honest, once they identified Victor Alvarado's body, the brother of the guy in your alley, they found he'd been missing a couple fingers, before he got hit by that semi." Reynolds waggled his eyebrows knowingly at Lou.

But Lou didn't know what that meant.

Circling his hand in between them, he continued. "Which is a sign the guy was in deep with some loan sharks. They most likely went after his brother, Frederick, once they realized Victor was dead and wouldn't be able to pay." Reynolds slapped his hands together like he was dusting them off. "Case closed. I mean, technically not. We'll still look into catching the loan guys, but they're a slippery bunch. It's likely East won't be able to find anything that'll stick in court with that lot. The important thing is this: there's nothing for you to worry about anymore."

Lou digested that information. She attempted to smile. "Thank you."

"Anytime." Reynolds went back to his screen.

But even though Officer Reynolds saw a tidy bow on the case, Lou couldn't help but feel like something was wrong. She held tight to the key in her pocket as she left the station.

There was only one way to find out if the key had belonged to Frederick. Using her phone, she searched his name and found an address in Tinsdale for his rare-books business. Then she called a car to drive her there.

If Easton was off for a couple of days, it was up to her to find out.

CHAPTER 13

Tinsdale was southeast of both Brine and Silver Lake, closest to the interstate. Willow hadn't exaggerated when she'd described the city as a ghost town. It was a shell.

Many of the homes appeared nice enough from the outside. The neighborhoods were quaint. But the business sector of the city was practically deserted. Large strip malls sat empty, their parking lots cracked and growing weeds. The shadows of old signs stained the buildings, reminders of what used to be.

Out the taxi window, a large, abandoned concrete structure loomed—that must've been the steel manufacturing plant Willow had mentioned. It was giant and could've easily employed the whole town. It certainly had been the life force of the city, because now that it was shut down, the place seemed to have been sucked dry.

"Here you are," said Lou's driver, pulling up to a deserted street. On the left side were some weather-worn houses with sad yards, and to her right was a business building with office spaces along the street level and apartments up above. The street ended at a deserted-looking train car depot station.

"Thank you." She paid and got out of the car, checking the address once more as the taxi pulled away.

The office spaces seemed mostly unused. A couple had boarded-up windows, while others had broken blinds covering the doors. Painted business names had been scratched off the windows and doors, all except a dentist's office at the end of the complex to her right, and an office in front of her that had a printed sign in the window. She moved closer to that sign, which announced it as *Frederick Alvarado - Rare Book Acquisitions.*

Lou studied the place, puzzled at the incongruities. The complex was nearly abandoned, and he'd just printed out a sign made with Microsoft Word. She screwed up her face as she tried to reconcile any of this with the well-dressed, frantic man she'd met so briefly last week. Shoving her hand into her pocket, Lou clutched the key, wondering if she was seriously about to break into a dead man's apartment.

But all of those plans fell flat when her attention landed on the door handle.

Instead of a regular lock, it held one of those numeric key pads, like many of the nicer places in New York, where people had moved to, so they didn't have to worry about keys. It was clear the dimple key didn't open this door.

Lou thought about Frederick, about his book business. There was something that told her this key was Frederick's, and if it didn't open his door, that meant it might open something inside.

Maybe she could crack his numeric code.

The thought overwhelmed her. Using a key to enter felt

different than using a keypad to gain entry, for some reason. The key code made it feel more like breaking and entering.

Lou took a walk around the block to think things through. She still had yet to see a soul but didn't want to look like a prowler if anyone was watching from inside the houses.

As she walked, she considered her options. *If* she could crack Frederick's code—and that was a big if—she was only going inside to find answers. She wouldn't take anything. The police had already been inside and had gotten everything they could from the place, so it wasn't as if she might ruin evidence. Thinking of the police reminded her of Easton. Maybe she should just wait until he was back on duty.

But Frederick had left the key with her as if he knew she was the one person who would know what to do with it.

Lou turned the corner around the backside of the building. Even the air smelled different here. Whereas scents of cinnamon and waffle cones swirled through the street of Button, Tinsdale simply smelled flat, cold, and metallic. There were no cars driving by or shoppers walking down the street. Even the train tracks across the way were void of movement, with only a few empty train cars sitting in the lot.

She rounded the next corner and thought about Ben. What would he have done in this situation? A smile pulled at her lips as she got her answer in the form of a memory. She'd sat in on one of his freshman classes once, and Ben had stood in the front of the lecture hall, larger than life, urging the students to use their minds to wonder and question.

"Take Eleanor Roosevelt's advice and treat your curiosity as the most useful gift you were endowed with," he'd said and then had sent a sly wink toward Lou.

She was curious about the key enough that she owed it to herself to try. Rounding the last corner, Lou walked toward

Frederick's apartment again, determined. Her curiosity over-whelmed her as she studied the keypad on the front door.

If he was a book lover like her, she might be able to figure it out. On her first try, she pressed the numbers four-five-one and then clicked the lock button. Maybe he was a *Fahrenheit 451* fan.

It clicked at her, flashing red.

It might be a four-digit code, she realized, clicking in six-four-five-one, replacing the F with a six since it was the sixth letter in the alphabet. Still, the red light flashed at her.

The next time, she tried one-nine-eight-four for George Orwell's classic and three-two-two for *Catch-22*. Two clicks. Two red flashes.

It was then that she remembered Frederick's mention of Diana Moon Glampers. Maybe it was more than just a coinci-dental mention. Maybe he was really into Vonnegut. Lou thought about important numbers surrounding the eccentric author. There was *Slaughterhouse-Five*, of course, but the number five wasn't enough for a security code, and converting all the letters in slaughterhouse to numbers would make it too long.

What about spelling out the word five? Lou counted in her head as she stood there. Five converted into numbers repre-senting their place in the alphabet would give her six, nine, twenty-two, and five. That was five digits. She tried it anyway. The machine clicked and flashed red, just like the last few times.

Glancing around at the empty sidewalk, Lou confirmed she was still alone. But the more time she stood out here, the more attention she drew. Pulling out her phone, she called the number George had given her when she'd bought the security cameras.

"George here," the young woman answered. The sound of plastic clicking and sound effects in the background told Lou that she was most likely sitting in that chair playing video games, just like she had been when Lou and Noah had visited her shop.

"Hi, George. This is Lou Henry." Lou paused, then added, "The new girl in town. You sold me security cameras."

"Sure," George said. "They acting up on you?"

"No. They're great. I'm calling with a weird tech question. I thought you might be able to answer." Lou wet her lips, unsure how much she should tell George.

Technically, what she was doing was trying to break into someone's apartment. Even if the inhabitant was deceased, it was still against the law.

"Sure. I live for weird tech questions." George chuckled. The sounds in the background stopped as if Lou had her full attention after that statement.

"Do you carry any of those front door locks that have a keypad?" Lou asked, deciding to start there.

"I have a couple of models. You want one for your place?" George asked.

"Not exactly. I'm actually trying to open someone else's." Lou waited. When she didn't hear any gasping or other signs that her statement had scandalized George, she added, "I have some guesses, but I'm not sure how many numbers to try. Do they usually have a limit?"

"What brand is it?" George asked, not missing a beat.

Lou read the brand off the keypad.

George whistled. "That's a good one. Really secure."

Heart sinking at George's words, Lou was about to give up hope.

"While a lot of them have four-digit codes, the better ones

go up to nine, so it's harder to guess." George was silent for a beat. "One thing you can do is check to see if any of the buttons are more worn than the others."

Lou peered at the keypad. "The only key that seems faded is the two."

"If he bought this brand, it's safe to say the guy didn't just make a nine-digit code of all twos," George said with a snort. "But it could mean that his code contains multiple twos."

"Okay, thank you." Lou looked up at the sky as she thought.

"No problem. Good luck." George ended the call.

Something that has a lot of twos in it and possibly has to do with Kurt Vonnegut, Lou mused.

She was about to walk around the building again while she thought when the answer hit her. There was a short story of Vonnegut's that Ben used to use during his Shakespeare unit. What had the title been? It was a chilling look at the theme of suicide in *Hamlet* with the addition of Vonnegut's feelings about population control. The answer came to her, and she snapped her fingers. It had been titled *2 B R 0 2 B*.

"Two B or naught two B," Lou whispered to herself.

She took a moment and changed the Bs to twos and the R to an eighteen in her mind. Fingers trembling in anticipation, she tried two-two-one-eight-zero-two-two. That had to be right. There were so many twos.

The lock clicked. The light flashed red.

Frustration rose inside her. How was that wrong? She'd been so sure. Lou tried to remember more about the short story. Had she gotten something wrong?

Lou squeezed her eyes shut and remembered Ben explaining it to her for the first time. He wore a huge grin as he spoke, like he did whenever he discussed Vonnegut.

"If people don't want to live anymore, that's the number they call, 2BR02B," Ben had said.

A phone number, not letters in the alphabet. Heartbeat quickening, she pulled up her phone function and checked the number pad to see where the B and the R fell on the numeric pad.

Exhaling first, Lou tried the code two-two-seven-zero-two-two. She waited.

The lock clicked. It flashed green.

Lou jumped in surprise. She felt like celebrating, but she didn't have time. Her hands scrambled with the handle as she opened the door and slipped inside.

The space was meticulously kept, though sparse. The hard-wood floors were sorely in need of refinishing, but they were clean. The walls were bare, painted a stark white, the bottom half covered with gray wainscoting. In the middle of the room, a desk sat on an antique rug.

But then there were the books. Shelves lined each wall. Tall antique bookshelves held ornate books, some of which probably belonged in a museum, they were so well preserved. Fabric covers, gilt-edged pages, gold lettering. All of it flashed into Lou's peripheral vision as she took in the room. Her gaze roamed among titles. She wasn't anything close to being a rare bookdealer, so she didn't know what any of it was worth, but she had a feeling that Frederick had been rather good at what he did, based on the collection he'd amassed.

Details jumped out at her as she scanned the room. The books were arranged by author last name and then alphabetically by title. A film of black powder rested along most of the surfaces. That, added to the few things in the room that were out of place, confirmed the police had documented the scene. She moved on with her own inspection.

The desktop was neat, with a nice computer sitting on it. The cords ran along the back, the first thing someone would see walking in. *Not necessarily the greatest greeting to customers,* Lou mused. *Then again, neither was the Word-printed sign in the window.*

It all made sense, however, when Lou noticed a stack of mailing supplies next to the desk. Frederick didn't have this space as a shop for customers to visit, his business must've taken place mostly over the internet. He would locate books and mail them out to his customers. So it really didn't matter what the space looked like or how run down the building was. As long as Frederick didn't mind, it wouldn't affect his sales one bit.

The itching need to confirm her theory crept along her fingers, making them tingle. She pulled out her phone and checked for a website. It was very well done, professional-looking and tasteful.

From the suit he'd been wearing, to the quality of the books inside, and the small touches like the expensive door lock, Lou felt confident that Frederick really had done well for himself. He merely spent money on things that were important to him and didn't worry about the rest.

After a quick scan of the downstairs space, Lou crept upstairs. There was a lonely, but neat, full-sized bed. A small kitchenette was positioned in the corner next to a couch. There was a tiny bathroom, and that was it. As was the case below, there were nice items in the minimalist space. Another book-shelf took up the wall space next to the bed, and the couch was a tasteful gray tweed that seemed like a cozy place to curl up with a book. The same black powder covered surfaces upstairs, showing the police had been thorough. Cabinet doors remained opened from where they must've searched, and

Frederick's mattress was askew, the crisp sheets had been pulled back.

Lou went back downstairs and dug into her pocket for the key. "What do you open?" she asked it, an action that made about as much sense as talking to the cats in her bookshop.

She went around to the front of the desk, searching for a locked drawer, but it was just a desk, no storage. Moving to study the bookshelves, she checked for any cupboards. But there were none. There wasn't a hidden keyhole in any of the ornately carved wood along the edges of each shelf.

Lou scanned for a safe or file cabinet in the corners of the room, to no avail. She returned upstairs but was met with the same results. Tapping the key in a slower, more measured imitation of Frederick's tapping that day in her bookshop, Lou wracked her brain.

The key might not open anything here. Frederick might have another house, or a storage locker somewhere, but Lou had a feeling it was here. She just needed to look in the right place.

Her mind returned to the Vonnegut passcode to the front door. She raced over to the bookshelf by his bed, assuming it was his personal collection. There were multiple copies of Vonnegut books, but they were definitely more of the well-loved variety. His paperback of *Slaughterhouse-Five* was creased and the spine cracked. The copies of *Hocus Pocus* and a compilation of Vonnegut's short stories were the same.

She moved all of them from side to side, pulling them out, but there were no hidden compartments or false backs to the shelves. Defeated, she headed back downstairs. She was scanning the titles on the first shelf when her phone rang. Lou answered it, seeing it was Willow.

"I just left school for the day and I'm heading to the store.

What do you feel like for dinner? Spaghetti or soup?" Willow asked, the sounds of a car starting in the background.

"Uh …" Lou didn't know what to say. She hadn't realized it was close to three in the afternoon.

"Or we could do something else if those options don't sound good," Willow said, misinterpreting her friend's silence.

Lou blinked. "No, it's just …" She pressed her lips together for a quick second, hoping Willow wouldn't be mad at her for what she was about to tell her. "I'm in Frederick's house at the moment, in Tinsdale, so I can't really think straight."

"What?" Willow stage-whispered even though Lou was sure she was alone in her car. "And you didn't invite me?"

Of course that would be Willow's only concern. Not the breaking of laws. "You were at work. I found a key that I think he left in the bookshop. Well, Romeow found it."

"And it was the key to his house? Oh man. That's so cool." Willow's voice went all high pitched.

"Not exactly. In fact, I'm still looking for what it opens. I got inside because he has a numeric keypad, and I guessed his code." Lou started inspecting the titles again as she talked to Willow.

"Only you," Willow said with a chuckle. "I feel like I should be scared of your detail-oriented mind, sometimes, but instead I'm just intrigued. Do you need backup?" she asked, but a blinker sounded, and Lou could tell she was already making the turn to come that way.

"Sure." Lou laughed. It would be good to talk through the possibilities. Maybe she was missing something. She gave Willow directions to the place and hung up.

Lou cringed as she went to pull some books off the shelf. Frederick's personal selection of books upstairs had been less fancy than these, and she didn't have enough rare-books experience to know if even a bit of dirt or oil from a person's skin would have a big effect on their quality or price.

She pulled her sweater sleeves down over her hands and used them as makeshift gloves to move the books.

On the third shelf, she noticed a collection of Kurt Vonnegut books. They were expensively bound and screamed "collector's editions." Carefully pulling one out at a time, she studied them. Maybe the key opened a lock on a fake book that held the secret to his death?

That's probably a little too Cloak and Dagger, she thought to herself with a snort.

But she stopped short when she was about to put the copy of *Cat's Cradle* back. At the back of the bookshelf was a black ribbon. Lou placed the book on the desk behind her and pulled at the ribbon.

She tugged until she felt a release. A click followed over to her left.

Lou moved over toward the wall. The wainscoting stretched all the way to the stairs. She ran her finger over the painted wooden boards, stopping when she felt one sticking up higher than the previous slats. Inspecting it closer, she noticed a gap between the wall and the panel. Prying it with her fingers, she pulled the panel out like a small door. It swung toward her.

The opening revealed a large metal container sitting in between the wooden studs of the wall. Lou's eyes locked on to the front where a combination lock sat above a handle. At the top of the handle, there was a keyhole. Fumbling with the key in her excited state, Lou finally pushed it into the lock and turned.

The safe clicked open.

CHAPTER 14

The metal door swung toward Lou with an eerie creak that caused a shiver to run down her spine. She leaned closer to get a look at what it held.

Inside, she found a dusty cardboard box full of books, sitting on top of everything, as if someone had shoved it inside in a hurry. The books inside were an odd assortment of titles. *The Hobbit, Charlie and the Chocolate Factory,* and *The Hound of the Baskervilles* joined other classics. Pulling the box of books out, she set it aside so she could get a better view of what lay underneath. Also, inside the metal container were stacks of money. She'd been right, Frederick had done well for himself.

There was another copy of *Slaughterhouse-Five.* But unlike Frederick's creased paperback upstairs, this one was in pristine condition. Inside, the copyright page confirmed it was a first edition, and Vonnegut's signature graced the title page. He'd drawn the same cartoon of his face—complete with a pointy nose, mustache, and curly hair—around the signature that Lou had seen in some of Ben's books.

As she set the Vonnegut book back inside, an envelope

caught her eye. She pulled it out and opened it to find a hand-written letter. The handwriting was beautiful, a curling script that spoke of hours of practice. But as Lou scanned the words, she realized they were anything but beautiful.

Freddie,

Just so you're aware, I know what you're up to. I'm waiting until the perfect moment to expose you. I can't believe you thought you could get away with something like this. I'm two steps ahead of you, until the day you die.

Eloise

Lou jumped in surprise as a knock came at the front door. She almost dropped the letter before turning to see Willow standing outside.

In her excitement over finding the hidden compartment, she'd forgotten Willow was on her way. Racing over to the door, Lou let her friend inside and checked the street to make sure no one was watching. As had been the case when she'd first arrived, the streets were still empty, hauntingly quiet.

"I cannot believe you broke into a dead guy's apartment." Willow stood still as if refusing to move until her friend answered for her uncharacteristic actions.

"I know." Lou's eyes dropped to the floor. She glanced up at Willow guiltily. "Easton is off duty, and I just had to know if this key opened anything. Ben always said curiosity was our most useful gift, and so I embraced my curiosity." She shrugged.

Willow laughed. "I'm not sure if this is what Ben meant. Are you sure you're feeling okay?"

Lou didn't have the brain space to chitchat. "I'm fine. Come here. I found something. There was a hidden container in the wall." She dragged her friend over to the box of books and the menacing letter from the person called Eloise.

"Yikes." Willow's eyebrows jumped up on her forehead as she scanned the letter. "This lady had it in for our dear Freddie."

Lou pulled out a book from the box that had been in the safe, trying to ascertain why they'd been stored in there, away from the rest of his collection. She flipped through the first few pages, then froze.

"I'm not sure Freddie was so dear," Lou said, motioning to the box of books she'd only glanced at before. Pulling out another, she confirmed it was the same. "It looks like these are all faked first editions."

"How can you tell?" Willow asked.

Lou pointed to the copyright page of the book she held. "The text *First Edition* is in a slightly different font, and see how the ink is a little darker, like they've added it after the fact. Look at the difference with this one." She showed Willow the real first edition of *Slaughterhouse-Five* she'd been admiring earlier for comparison.

"I wouldn't have noticed that," Willow scoffed.

"Only people in the book business would." Lou glanced at the print number. "But I'd bet if we check these print numbers, they wouldn't match the first-edition printing runs, which means they're fakes."

Willow tsked. "Oh, Frederick. What did you get into? You think this is what killed him?"

"I don't know. The policeman I talked to today said they're all convinced Frederick's brother, Victor, owed a lot of money to loan sharks, who must've gone after Frederick for the money after they found out Victor was dead." Lou sighed. None of that fit together in her mind.

She flipped to the previous page in the book she held and gasped. Placed inside was a bookmark. At the top it held the Button Books logo with a place underneath for the price and a handwritten note, *First Edition*. Lou showed Willow.

"These came from my shop," she said, her voice shaking. "I've seen these bookmarks in the rare books they didn't want to put a price sticker on, like the regular used books."

"I can't imagine Nina getting involved in something like this," Willow said, mentioning Kimberly's aunt, who'd owned the shop for decades before she passed away and left it to her niece. "Kimberly? Now that, I can imagine."

Lou checked the other books while Willow talked. All of them held the same bookmark. Lou thought of the threatening phone message she'd gotten. "I think you're right about Kimberly being involved in this. I think she and Frederick might have been working together."

Clicking her tongue, Willow said, "Whatever happened, this Eloise character really hated Frederick." She read over the beautifully handwritten note full of such ugly words. Then she turned to Lou. "Wait, you said you talked to a policeman earlier, but Easton's out of town." She placed a hand on her hip. "Come to think of it, I need you to explain everything that led to you breaking into a dead guy's apartment."

Lou took the next few minutes doing just that. She explained the threatening voicemail, her trip to the police station, and what Officer Reynolds had told her. At the end of her story, her shoulders sank forward.

"What?" Willow asked, noticing her mood.

"How was I so wrong about Frederick's character? I got a good feeling about him when he came into my shop. Sure, he was frantic and worried, but he didn't seem like a bad guy."

She motioned to the faked first editions. "Not like someone who would dupe people." She winced.

Willow scratched at her nose. "I mean, you said he reminded you of Ben with that whole Glampers line. Maybe that clouded your judgment. You were feeling sentimental and missing Ben. You can't blame yourself for that."

Lou rubbed at her nose—the dust from the box tickled her nostrils. "I guess."

She put everything back into the hiding spot and locked it once more. The bookmark sitting inside each of the books made Lou feel sick to her stomach.

Stashing the key back in her pocket, she patted it. "I'll save this for Easton. He should go through all of this when he gets back." Lou motioned for the door. "Where is he, anyway?"

"I don't know. It's not like he would tell me," Willow said with a snort, "but he took his boat with him, so I'm guessing he went out to Silver Lake to do some fishing. That's where his parents live."

They slipped out of the front door and made a beeline for Willow's car. Once they were inside and on the road, Lou exhaled in relief.

"Okay, so let's go over what we know." Willow kept her focus on driving, but her mind was clearly on the case. "Frederick died Friday night in Button after showing up at the bookstore and asking for Kimberly, saying it was urgent."

"It's possible he needed to warn her that someone they sold a first edition to had found out it was fake and was after them," Lou suggested. "Do you think Frederick could've just put those bookmarks inside to place the blame elsewhere in case he got caught?"

"And then came racing to warn her when they were discovered because he felt bad?" Willow shrugged. "I don't know. If someone's callous enough to do that in the first place, they don't seem like the kind of person to come warn someone after the fact. Plus, knowing Kimberly for the year she was in town, I'd bet on her being involved in a scam every time over her being a victim. The woman got herself involved in a betting ring, two email scams, and even a multilevel marketing scheme all in the mere twelve months she lived in Button."

"Okay, so one explanation of what happened could be that she and Freddie were working together. What if she sold him out?" Lou's eyebrows lifted at her own idea. "She realized they were in trouble and cut out, leaving Frederick to deal with the consequences."

Willow tapped her hand on the steering wheel. "You know, that could be it. Remember the day you decided to buy the bookstore?"

Lou fiddled with Frederick's key in her pocket. "Yeah, you said you'd been there and had forgotten it was for sale."

"Because Kimberly reminded me when I was in that day," Willow said. "When she first put it up for sale after her aunt passed away, I mentioned how much of a shame it was that you and Ben couldn't buy it because it had always been your dream to own a bookshop, and that you had loved it each time you visited me. But Kimberly thought I was trying to negotiate and mentioned that she wouldn't budge on the price."

"Oh, I remember you telling me about that," Lou said with a chuckle.

Willow nodded. "But when I went in a month ago to buy a book for my nephew, Kimberly was acting all weird and desperate. She came up to me and asked me if my friend was still interested. I mentioned that you *had* actually been discussing a change. That's when she said she would take the price down twenty percent, to make it happen quickly."

Lou nodded along to the story. "She could've realized things were going south, and she needed to get out of there quickly. When I came in with an offer, she took it and ran. You said no one's seen her since the closing date, right?"

"Not a glimpse." Willow swallowed.

"Then there's the theory that the police have bought into," Lou said, "which is that the loan sharks that were after Victor, Freddie's little brother, and went after Freddie to cover Victor's outstanding debts."

"That doesn't make sense." Willow snorted. "Loan sharks take people's fingers and break their knees, right? If they kill someone, there's no way they're getting money out of them."

"Even if they only kill his brother and not the guy who owes them the money? Easton said it took the police a few days to find Victor's body. Maybe the loan sharks didn't know Victor was dead either," Lou said. She didn't like the theory but didn't want to count something out just because it didn't feel right to her.

Willow conceded. "I suppose that could've happened. It does seem rather unlikely, though."

"And then there's the stuff Frederick left behind in my shop to consider." Lou dropped her hand, unsure where that all fit. "He didn't know me at all. I thought he'd just forgotten that paper on the table because he left so quickly, but that key seemed to be hidden on the bookshelf on purpose."

"You said he ran out the back door, not the front door, right?" Willow asked.

Lou nodded.

"What if someone was chasing him?" Willow asked. "They showed up, and he had to run out the back. They were after the key, so he hid it in your shop and was going to come back for it later."

"Only he never could because the person who was after him killed him in the alley. Maybe they followed him back there." Lou shivered. "They could've run through my shop, and I didn't even know." She was even more thankful for her cameras at that moment.

"Or they ran around the outside and cut him off in the alley," Willow suggested.

Lou liked that idea only slightly more. It still meant there had been a person chasing Frederick when he'd come in to ask for help. And as much as Lou hated the idea that Frederick had been involved in something shady, like selling off fake first editions, it didn't mean he deserved to die.

"We need to find Kimberly," Willow said with conviction. "If she and Frederick were running a scam together, the same person who killed him could be after her."

"If they haven't already found her." Lou swallowed.

"Right." Willow tightened her fingers around the steering wheel. "Or if she wasn't the person who killed Frederick in the first place."

Lou's eyes widened. "You think Kimberly is capable of murder?"

Shrugging, Willow said, "When I was setting up the plants in front of your shop the other day and overheard the police officers talking about the tags in Frederick's suit, they mentioned a head wound. I think that's how he died."

"I didn't see any signs of a head wound." Lou leaned back in her seat.

"Exactly." Willow pointed at her. "Which means it was on the back of his head, the part we couldn't see when he was sitting up against the building like that."

"Which is also where a person might hit their head if they

were pushed or fell back," Lou reasoned as she followed Willow's line of thought.

"But Easton was ruling it a homicide because someone moved the body to sit up like that. That can't have been where he fell or else Easton wouldn't be so sure someone else was involved." Willow turned and they passed the Button welcome sign.

Even after only a week, the streets were already feeling like home to Lou. The feeling was such a dichotomous one to the eeriness that had arisen from their conversation, something that made her feel unsafe and wary.

"But it couldn't have been Kimberly who killed him," Lou said suddenly. When Willow glanced over at her, she added, "If Frederick had seen Kimberly, he wouldn't have run out the back door. He would've gone after her. He was searching for her, after all."

"Good point." Willow nodded. "Which means Kimberly's most likely not our murderer, but she might be in trouble too. We need to find her as soon as we can."

CHAPTER 15

After parking in downtown Button, Willow and Lou traveled from business to business, asking around about Kimberly. Not a soul had seen her nor heard from her since the day Lou closed on the bookshop.

Many of the locals they asked adopted the same worried expressions Lou and Willow wore as they asked about Kimberly. A few of the locals sneered and cursed the woman's name, citing something sketchy she'd tried to involve them in or an example of her rudeness.

They even stopped by the police station, leaving the key to Frederick's hidden container with a note for Easton. Lou explained where she found the key, that she believed it belonged to Frederick, and that she suspected he had been involved in a first edition scam, all of which might be important to the case. She hesitated to write any more than that on paper, not wanting to admit in writing that she'd trespassed, but vowed to fill in the rest of the blanks in person when Easton came back from his trip.

By the time Lou returned to the bookshop that evening, she

was beat. Collecting the cats, she herded them upstairs, hoping Romeow didn't do too much damage while he was up in the apartment alone. She hadn't expected to be gone most of the day.

A warm, clean apartment welcomed her and the other cats. Lou let her head fall back in relief. At least one thing had gone her way today. But any sense of contentment was short lived.

Just as Lou sat down with a book, her phone buzzed with another security alert. Clicking through to the live video feed, she hoped it was just a wandering raccoon or a bag blowing in the wind.

A hooded figure approached the back door, trying the handle, only to find it locked. Heartbeat ramping up like a high-speed roller coaster, Lou sat up and jumped out of bed. She stomped downstairs, grabbed her stun gun from the drawer, and threw on a jacket this time.

She didn't bother texting Easton, knowing he was out of town, but also feeling self-conscious now that she'd heard Officer Reynolds talk about her like she was hogging the detective's time and attention.

Plus, the first visitor had most likely been someone coming to look at the crime scene after the story about Frederick's death ran on the news. The second had been a man dropping off a cat he was too afraid to admit he didn't want to take care of anymore. This was probably something else just as innocent.

Taking a deep, fortifying breath, Lou swung open the back door after checking the video footage to make sure the person was far enough away from the door that she wouldn't hit them when it opened.

"Hey," she shouted. "What are you doing back here?"

This time, the person didn't freeze. There was no meowing. This time, they ran.

Gritting her teeth for a second, Lou ran after them. She had too many questions to let this person go without at least attempting to get answers. She patted her pocket to check she had her keys and slammed the back door shut, waiting until she heard the lock click.

The ground was slick with the beginnings of a nighttime frost, but she found her stride as she came out the other side of the alley and spotted a figure running down Lace Avenue.

"Stop," she called after them as she picked up her pace. "Come back."

But the person did neither.

It only took her another half block to catch up to them.

"Please. Stop. I just want to talk." The icy air burned in Lou's lungs as she ran level with the person. "Please," she repeated.

At the end of the block, instead of racing across Binding Street, the figure stopped. A hand came up and gripped the side of the building next to them. Their back heaved up and down with desperate breaths.

Lou kept her stun gun ready in her pocket as she waited. "Why were you lurking around my shop?" she asked.

The person turned to face her. It was a man, probably in his thirties, definitely out of shape. "You ... you're ... fast." He gasped out the words.

"I run," Lou said. "Now would you answer my question, please." It wouldn't help to forget her manners. It had been her last plea that seemed to make him stop after all.

He rubbed at his chest and winced. "I was looking for Kimberly, okay? I heard people around town say you knew where she was, so I was watching the place, trying to see if she showed up."

Kimberly. The town gossip mill must've distorted that

information. He'd heard she knew where Kimberly was instead of the truth.

"I don't know where she is; I'm searching for her too." Lou resisted the urge to throw her hands up in frustration.

Kimberly was becoming so much more of a thorn in Lou's side than she could've predicted. But through the overwhelming irritation gathering in her mind about the bookshop's former owner, concern peeked its way through.

"So you know Kimberly, then?" Lou asked the man, who was just now catching his breath.

"As much as anyone can." He narrowed his eyes at Lou. "What trouble do you think she's gotten into?"

Lou rubbed her hands up and down her arms. Even with a jacket, it was freezing out.

"Want to go inside? Get out of the cold?" The man gestured to the building behind them.

It was the Button Bistro. Candlelit tables with dim, romantic lighting emitted such a low glow, Lou hadn't even thought it was open. There was a couple sitting by the window. They stared at each other lovingly, completely oblivious to Lou and her mystery lurker. She liked the idea of going to a place with other people since she still didn't quite trust this man.

"Sure," she said, glancing down at her outfit. She wore black leggings and a wool sweater. Not her best clothes, but at least she hadn't changed into pajamas yet.

The man held the door open for her. As she passed by him, a pleasant laundry detergent smell wafted off his jacket. That was quickly overtaken by the smells inside. Rich garlicky butter smells mingled with the scent of crackling meats and cream-based sauces—Lou may have glimpsed the menu on the way inside. She'd also checked the business hours. It was past eight already, but they were open until ten.

After reading the *Seat Yourself* sign, she settled down at the table next to the couple by the window. Other than a server scuttling about, and a single chef in the back by the kitchen, they were the only other souls inside.

As Lou settled into a seat, the man took off his jacket and hung it on the back of his own chair. He removed the gray beanie he'd been wearing. Curly ash-brown hair sprang out in unruly ringlets, but instead of appearing unkempt, it was endearingly messy. Now that they were in better light, Lou could see he was around her age, if not a little younger. He had a wide mouth that when paired with his curly hair and blue eyes, made him look more like a movie star.

Holding his hand out, the man said, "I'm Quinn, by the way."

Lou shook his hand. "Lou. I bought the bookstore from Kimberly." Lou leaned forward. "The two of you are together?"

"I thought we were until I found out she'd been hanging out with her ex. I confronted her about it last week, and she's been ghosting me ever since." Quinn puffed out his cheeks in annoyance.

Lou worried that the reason Kimberly was ghosting Quinn had more to do with the Alvarado brother's deaths than her being mad, but she decided to keep that theory to herself.

A server came over at that moment. His red hair was pulled back into a ponytail, and he had a charming half smile that made it seem like he'd just told a joke and was waiting for a reaction. "What can I get you two?" he asked, brandishing two menus and a separate drink list.

It was too late for coffee, and Lou wanted to stay lucid

enough for the conversation. "I'll have a hot tea. Anything caffeine free is fine. No food for me."

"Lager," Quinn said to the man, with a nod.

"Coming right up." The server left, taking the menus with him.

Lou turned her attention back to Quinn. "Did Kimberly mention anything to you about selling fake first editions?" she asked.

Quinn's face creased into a frown. "Kimmie didn't tell me much about what she was doing. I was trying to help her figure out her finances, but I'm thinking she might be a lost cause."

"What about the name Frederick Alvarado?" Lou asked. "Did she ever mention him?"

At that, Quinn pushed his shoulders back, sitting up straight. "Not Frederick but her ex, the one I was telling you she'd gone back to recently, was named Victor Alvarado."

"That's Frederick's brother." Lou gasped. "So Victor and Kimberly were together." Thoughts swirled around Lou as she considered the implications this had for the case and the assumptions she had made about Frederick's death.

"Off and on for years, apparently." Quinn ran a hand through his curls. They sprung out from under his fingers. "She was trying to get away from him. Said he was a bad influence on her, but I'm not so sure it wasn't the other way around now."

"Or maybe they kept each other down," Lou mused, more to herself than Quinn.

"Could be." He scratched at his head.

The server came back, setting a frosty beer in front of Quinn and then a mug with a bag of chamomile tea and a small teapot of steaming water next to Lou. They thanked him, and Lou poured the hot water over the tea bag, letting it steep. The steamy air that billowed up from the mug caused her to shiver as one last chill from being out in the frosty night air moved through her.

"You think Victor got Kimmie into trouble again?" Quinn asked.

Lou lifted one shoulder, letting it drop. "Well, he's dead and so is his brother, who came into my shop last Friday asking for the previous owner. He was pretty frantic. I'm only guessing that Kimberly's involved since I haven't spoken to her."

"So that's what she meant." Quinn snorted.

"What?" Lou asked, taking a sip of her tea.

"I heard she was hanging out with Victor again," Quinn explained. "She got really upset when I confronted her about it, telling me it wasn't what I thought. Instead of explaining anything, she said she couldn't believe I didn't trust her and then kept muttering about how she didn't even know where the guy was."

Lou frowned at that information. "So she must've known he was missing and got worried."

Quinn shrugged. "The tough thing with Kimmie is that she always seemed worried. There was constantly someone after her, a payment she hadn't made, a place she couldn't show her face anymore. I got to thinking maybe she was making it all up."

"It sounds like Victor was in trouble with some loan sharks." Lou studied Quinn as she talked. "Do you think Kimberly could be in trouble, too, and she ran because she didn't want to get hurt?"

"It's not out of the question," Quinn said, exhaling a humorless laugh at the prospect. "I hate that I still worry about her, though. She left me, hasn't answered any of my calls or texts. Why can't I just let her go?"

Lou felt sorry for the man sitting across from her. She felt a big-sister kind of tenderness toward the guy. He could very well be lying to her, so she wasn't going to take anything he said as a fact, but he didn't seem like a bad person. From what she could see, his one mistake was getting tangled up with someone who was constantly in trouble.

The problem was, Lou couldn't yet decide if Kimberly was more of a victim or an active participant in the dangers surrounding her.

"Can you give me a list of the places Kimberly usually hangs out at?" Lou asked, pulling out her phone.

Quinn nodded. "I've been checking the Westmore and The Black Cat. They're her two favorite bars in Kirk." He laughed. "I've even checked the Boot Barn, her favorite shoe store. There's also By a Thread. It's a vintage shop. She used to spend a lot of time there. Said she had to dig to find the deals." He noticed Lou had typed those in and was waiting for more. "Other than that, she loved going to the Kirk Public House. It's a restaurant. And she got her hair done at Ashton's. It seemed like she was there every other week."

Lou typed those in as well. "Thank you." She checked the time. "It's getting late. I should head back." They exchanged numbers in case either of them heard from Kimberly.

Finishing her tea, she paid and left Quinn. Lou pondered the situation as she walked back to the bookshop in the moonlight.

Thinking back to that Friday evening when Frederick came into the shop, Lou wondered if he'd known his brother was dead. Easton said Victor had died a couple of days before Frederick. He could've been worried about his brother and had come looking for him at Kimberly's shop if they were in an on-again, off-again relationship.

Then what did the fake first editions have to do with anything? Lou wondered.

The icy night felt as if it were closing in on her as she walked. The more she learned about the man who'd died in her alley, the less sense it all made.

As much as she wanted to believe it had been the loan sharks, like Easton believed, Lou had a terrible feeling the violence wasn't over and that she'd been inadvertently pulled into harm's way.

CHAPTER 16

The whole next day, as Lou worked in the shop, she couldn't seem to let go of the nagging feeling that she was missing something.

There was something off about those fake first editions Frederick had hidden in his shop, and Lou wanted answers. She figured the best place to find them was by talking with the other booksellers who'd known Frederick. So after Willow was done with school that day, they drove out to Silver Lake to go question Lance Swatek again. She wasn't sure if Easton had ever looked into him, but she felt sure he would know more than they did about what Frederick had gotten himself into.

Lance was wearing the same worn baseball cap as the last time they'd seen him, but this time he had on a green, hooded sweatshirt. He glanced up, and his eyes narrowed with recognition as they walked inside.

"Back again?" Lance asked.

Lou steeled her resolve. "Back for the truth this time."

Willow crossed her arms and cocked an eyebrow.

"You said you didn't recognize the man in the sketch we

showed you last time, but you knew him, didn't you? His name is Frederick." Lou observed the effect of her words as Lance listened.

He moved to take off his baseball cap, but stopped. His eyes flicked up to meet Lou's, and he placed the cap back on his head without his usual scratching motion.

Lou could tell the man was going to try to lie or squirm his way out of it, so she wanted to cut the pretense and let him know they had caught him. "I saw you and a woman talking about him on Saturday at the book swap. She knew who he was."

Clearing his throat, he said, "Okay, so I know Frederick. Why's that a problem?"

"Because he's dead, and you seemed happy he was gone." Willow leaned in closer, attitude leaking from her tight posture.

"And you made yourself seem guilty by lying about not recognizing him," Lou added.

The shock written on Lance's face made Lou's conviction stumble.

"So that's why the detective asked me about Friday night," Lance muttered.

Lou perked up. Easton really had followed up on the clue. But the detective hadn't pursued him enough to tell him what happened to Frederick. That meant Lance must have a good alibi.

"Where *were* you Friday night?" Willow asked.

Lance held up his hands. "Hey, I was visiting my mom at the Alzheimer's care facility. There are records of me coming and going, as well as camera footage."

Lou tapped her fingers on her leg. If Easton had stopped the line of questioning at his alibi, that meant the time of death had been during the window Lance was visiting his mother. Which also meant that he wasn't Frederick's killer.

"Do you know anything about a woman named Eloise?" Willow asked, obviously recognizing the dead end at the same time Lou had.

At this, Lance's expression turned stone cold. "Eloise? Unfortunately." He scowled.

"Unfortunately?" Lou asked.

"What's she like?" Willow tacked on, leaning forward.

He let out a humorless laugh. "How do I describe Eloise?" His lips curled with disgust. "Have you ever met a person who you were sure had no soul?"

The women raised their eyebrows at the crass rhetorical question.

"No?" Lance said with a hollow laugh. "Hmm … what about someone who probably uses her spare time to guard the gates of hell?"

Okay, now the man is just being dramatic, Lou thought with an inward eye roll.

"I'm not," Lance said, holding up a hand, "exaggerating, if that's what you're thinking."

Lou frowned in surprise at how well he'd read her thoughts.

"She's another used bookdealer in the area, and she employs the most chilling tactics you'd ever think imaginable to get access to the pieces she acquires. Frederick seemed to have an annoying streak of luck, putting him in the way of amazing pieces all the time. He was easy to hate. At least he came about it honestly. Eloise? She's a whole different story."

Lance's mention of Frederick's honesty intrigued her. He obviously didn't know about the collection of fake first editions he'd been trying to pawn off on his customers. But

Frederick had hidden them in that safe, so there probably weren't many people who knew.

Lou's mind returned to the letter Eloise had written to Frederick. *I can't believe you thought you could get away with something like this.* Had she found out about the first editions?

From the sound of it, the woman wasn't squeaky clean either, though. Lou couldn't see her confronting Frederick or killing him over it. Unless …

"Did you, Frederick, and Eloise ever buy books from each other?" Lou asked.

Willow sucked in a breath, catching where Lou was going with the line of questioning.

Lance shrugged. "We try not to, though it has happened from time to time."

Excitement rose inside Lou. If Eloise had purchased a fake first edition from Frederick, that could've been grounds for her to confront him outside Lou's bookshop.

"You should ask her yourself, though." Lance said. "Didn't you say you talked to her at the book swap?"

Lou leaned back. "I didn't say that. We've never met Eloise."

"Yes, you have." Lance nodded. "The woman I was talking to, the one you said you heard me discussing Frederick with. That was Eloise."

"The old woman?" Lou blurted.

Lance spat out a laugh. "Oh, she's not a regular old woman. She's stronger than she looks." When the women gave him a questioning glare, he added, "She teaches kickboxing at the local Y on the weekends, and the deal she has with the devil probably keeps her young too." He shrugged.

Willow glanced over at Lou. A woman who taught kick-boxing and was obviously upset enough with Frederick to send him that strongly worded letter might've pushed him hard enough that he'd hit his head in Lou's alley.

And whereas Lou had told Easton about Lance, she hadn't gotten the chance to mention Eloise's letter or anything else she'd found in the safe since he was still out of town. She'd left him that note at the station but was sure it was still sitting on his desk along with the key, untouched.

"You said she employs 'chilling tactics' to acquire books. What did you mean by that?" Willow asked, leaning her elbows on the counter.

Lance scratched at his nose. "You didn't hear this from me, but kickboxing isn't the only class she teaches at the Y. She also has a SitFit Silver class where she does chair-based workouts with seniors." Lance scowled. "It's not what you think, though. She only does that so she can get close to these people before they die. They talk about her nonstop, so if they happen to … pass"—his nostrils flared—"their families usually reach out to her. She gets an invitation to their estate sale before the rest of us and nabs all the best books. A couple times, she's convinced their families a book was worthless only to turn around and sell it for hundreds or even thousands."

Discomfort squirmed up Lou's arms at the description of such shady tactics.

"And that's not her only hustle. She goes to art galleries, bookstores, even finds victims in the grocery store. She can befriend an older person like that." Lance snapped his fingers together. "Before you know it, they're inviting her over for dinner, and she's making a list of the rare books in their collection while she's supposed to be in the bathroom."

"She scouts out the books they have before they even pass away?" Willow asked in disgust.

Lance snorted. "I told you. She's awful, and that's just the stuff I'm sure about. I have my suspicions that she's helped a few of them to the grave, but I can't prove anything. She's probably the most awful person I've ever had the displeasure of meeting, and she's my competition. Add in Frederick, and you can see what I was up against."

Lou folded her arms. "So you didn't get rid of him because he was your competition?"

A groan spilled out of Lance. "Believe me. If either of them was going to go, I would've offed Eloise a long time ago. With my luck, she killed Frederick and is after me next."

"You think she could've killed Frederick?" Lou asked, thinking about the threatening letter she'd found.

Lance's eyes narrowed seriously. "Yeah. If I've ever met anyone who I think could be a killer, it would be Eloise." The man shivered. "I wouldn't be surprised, in the least, if the police found she had a bunch of bodies stored in a basement freezer or something."

Willow let out a low whistle. "Whoa."

"Do you know if she had any recent fights with Frederick or had any reason to hurt him?" Lou asked, searching for something more concrete than Lance's obvious disdain for the woman.

Squinting at the ceiling, Lance thought about that. "At the book swap, she mentioned him going on a last-minute trip. She was acting pretty smug about it, as if she'd had something to do with it."

Willow and Lou shared a pointed look. A trip? Or more like a fall?

"But she was sure he would've been back by the swap." Lance rotated the brim of his baseball hat to one side and then back. "She was just as surprised as I was that he wasn't there."

That information deflated Lou's suspicions slightly. It

146

sounded like this Eloise character was quite the actor, though. If she could make people believe she cared about them enough to be included in their end-of-life planning, she could surely fool Lance into thinking she had been expecting Frederick to show up at the book swap, even if she knew he wouldn't be there.

The only way to find out was to go talk to her, Lou decided.

"What's her shop name?" Lou asked, readying her phone to type his reply in her search bar.

"Pages," Lance said with a snort. "It's a used bookstore in Kirk."

Lou and Willow thanked Lance for the information and walked outside.

"We need to go find Eloise and see if she has an alibi for Friday night." Willow grabbed her car keys out of her messenger bag.

"Agreed. Easton may have already cleared Lance, but he doesn't even know about Eloise yet. Should we call him?" Lou asked, turning back to her friend. Willow was frozen. Her expression filled with dread. "Look," Lou said softly, "I know you're not crazy about the guy, but he's the lead detective on this case, and if he's in Silver Lake already, maybe we should invite him to meet us. We could all go to Eloise's store together."

Willow didn't seem to hear any of what Lou was saying; her gaze was focused past Lou, over her shoulder. Lou turned and realized there had been a good reason for Willow's reaction.

The last person they wanted to see was walking straight toward them.

CHAPTER 17

Willow and Lou stood frozen on the sidewalk in Silver Lake, but their lack of movement had nothing to do with the freezing temperatures outside.

It had everything to do with Willow's ex-fiancé striding toward them, his arm wrapped around his new girlfriend's shoulders.

James Tippery was a handsome man, if you didn't know the real him. He was the type of guy who fooled people into thinking he was nice but eventually showed his true ugliness if you stuck around him long enough. Fortunately for Willow, she'd found out before she walked down the aisle with the guy. Unfortunately, she'd still wasted years with him, and her broken heart would most likely take even longer to heal.

Lou stood in front of Willow, reaching back to grab her friend's hand. It was just like Willow had done back in middle school, when she'd punched Greg Olsen in the nose for spreading rumors about Lou after she'd dumped him. Lou's fingers curled into a fist. She'd never hit anyone in her life, but she thought she might break that streak for James.

His brown eyes lit up as bright as a competitive neighborhood Christmas display as he homed in on Willow and Lou. He was tall, which was part of what had attracted Willow to him. Lou knew she regretted that now that she'd seen his true character.

The woman James had his arm around must be Tiffany Wentz, Lou guessed, since she'd only ever heard Willow describe her over the phone. She was petite—even shorter than Lou, who stood at five foot four—and had big, bouncy brown hair. She had to be a good foot shorter than James.

Willow wasn't a petty person. She'd dated many men who were the same height or even shorter than her. While she loved the idea of feeling smaller than her horses, she'd confided in Lou that she wasn't about to throw out a good relationship just because she was taller than a man. But when she'd found James, she thought she'd hit the jackpot. He was sweet, smart, successful, and six foot three—a good few inches taller than the willowy Willow. He managed the local bank and was close to his family.

They'd met during a fundraiser for the new high school track and had gotten engaged a year later. James and Willow bought the farmhouse on Spool Avenue together, actually. That had been yet another thing Willow loved about him; he'd insisted that OC was too important not to be part of their day-to-day living. They needed a place where there was enough land to keep him.

Two years later, when they still hadn't set a date for the wedding, Willow didn't mind. They were happy, or so she thought. That all came crashing down about six months ago when Willow found him and Tiffany together in his office at the bank.

Willow broke it off and bought him out of his part of the house using a loan from her parents that she was still paying off, and it was history. Except that it wasn't because he and Tiffany still lived in Button, still worked at the bank together, and still flaunted their relationship in Willow's face whenever they got the chance.

And now she wasn't even safe in neighboring cities either.

"Willow, how are you?" James asked as they approached, threading his fingers through Tiffany's. "It's been a while."

Willow cringed through a smile. "Not long enough, I'd say." She tipped her head toward Tiffany.

"We're house hunting," Tiffany said with a squeal, jumping up and down once before realizing that she probably shouldn't do that in heels. "James is buying me a house as a wedding present. Isn't that sweet?"

Willow coughed in surprise.

"Wedding present?" Lou asked, hoping her question covered for her friend.

Tiffany proffered her left hand and wiggled her delicate fingers. A large diamond ring sparkled on her finger. It was *so* large that Lou wondered how Tiffany could even lift her hand. Like, the woman really should watch out for crows and other creatures who are attracted to sparkly objects. It was *that* big.

"We've found a few we really like in the Montlake neighborhood," Tiffany went on.

From the way Willow's eyes widened, Lou guessed the neighborhood Tiffany had just mentioned was very expensive.

"The kitchen in the last one was to die for, wasn't it, baby?" Tiffany gazed up adoringly at James, her fingers twining their way around the zipper pull on his jacket.

Lou gritted her teeth as Willow became transfixed with the motion.

Either this Tiffany woman was as dense as a two by four, and didn't realize why anything she was saying would offend Willow, or she was an evil mastermind who found joy in rubbing her relationship in Willow's face.

"Well, we've got places to be." Lou linked her arm through her best friend's and tugged her down the street.

Once they'd put at least a block in between them—and Lou did a few checks over her shoulder to make sure the couple was out of sight—Willow deflated. Her tall body crumpled onto the nearest bench. Lou sat next to her.

"I'm so sorry." Lou wrapped an arm around her friend and held her tight. "Honest three."

"Angry. Disgusted. Brokenhearted." Willow let her head drop forward. Moving it back and forth in agony, she said, "Why does it bother me? It shouldn't. I hate him. I know I can do better than him."

"Because you were engaged," Lou reasoned in soft tones. "You were planning a life with him before he showed his true colors. That doesn't just go away overnight. It hurts. And even when wounds heal, we are still reminded of them by the scars they leave behind."

Lou felt Willow's body relax as she spoke. The tension left her, though not completely.

Willow peeked over at Lou and sniffed. "Look at me. I'm falling apart about a dumb cheater, but it's all so trivial compared to everything you've been through."

"Pain is pain," Lou said. "Just because we've had different painful things happen, doesn't mean you're not allowed to feel yours. This is hard. Give yourself a hand for getting through it."

Willow sat up straight. "Right. Okay, I'm good. We can go see Eloise now." She swiped at her misty eyes.

Lou studied her best friend. As much as she wanted to find Eloise and get some answers to their many questions, she knew her friend needed a break more than anything at that moment.

"Or we could visit Eloise tomorrow. Why don't we go somewhere fun for dinner? We're here in a big city," Lou said, a teasing grin peeling across her face. "Why don't we use the time to have a night on the town?"

Willow laughed. Silver Lake couldn't have had a population of much over ten thousand, but compared to Button, it felt positively urban.

"There is a really fun restaurant that makes amazing New Orleans food just down the street," Willow said with an increasing smile.

Lou got to her feet and held a hand out to help Willow up as well. "Perfect. And while we eat, we can plan all the terrible ways we hope karma gets back at James for the awful things he did to you."

Willow took her hand. "I hope he gets an ingrown toenail and can't wear the fancy loafers he loves because of the pain," she said, hooking her arm through Lou's as she got to her feet.

"Oh," Lou said with a laugh, "what about the house they buy has a secret termite infestation?"

Willow nodded. "That's a good start. Keep going."

As it turned out, Willow didn't want to discuss James at dinner that night. After listing only a few terrible wishes and an appetizer of crawdads, she turned the subject toward the bookshop.

"Do you know when you're going to open up for business?" Willow asked.

Lou let the question settle over her. "I mean, I feel like I'm getting close. I think I could open sooner than I first thought, maybe as early as next week. But I'd be lying if I said I wasn't more than a little scared. Terrified might be more like it. I'm not sure changing the name and signs will be enough to clean up the shop's reputation."

Willow put a hand on Lou's arm and squeezed tight. "You're the most capable, bookish person I know. Anything you do will be great." She took a crawdad from the basket and tilted her head. "But if you really want the town behind you, I think I have an idea."

"What's that?" Lou asked.

"What if you spruced up the place a bit by using some of the local businesses?" Willow suggested. "That way you can get the word out around town about your rebranding while supporting them."

Lou leaned forward. "I'm listening."

"Well, that seating area in the middle is pretty dusty and old," Willow said. "What if you had The Upholstered Button furnish that spot for you?"

Lou liked the idea. She had been wondering if cleaning the pieces would be enough to make them shine again. She really wanted that area to be a magnet to her shoppers, begging them to sit and curl up with a good book and a cat.

"I think that sounds great," she said. "And I can donate the old set. What else?"

"The Antique Button has some really great lamps. Maybe you could grab a few to spruce up the place as well as changing out those bulbs that are burnt out." Willow gave Lou a pointed look, proving she'd noticed Lou had been putting off that task.

Lou pulled out her phone and started a list. "I know I need to change those bulbs, I just don't have a ladder tall enough."

"I'm sure Noah does," Willow said with a wave of her hand. "Ask him."

Making a note, Lou got another idea. "The bakery could make cupcakes with little books and cats on top that I could serve on my opening night," Lou suggested.

"That's perfect. People love that kind of stuff. Especially with the weird press you got around Frederick's murder and the possibility that Kimberly was involved in that first-edition scam, I think you're really going to want to hit the *new owner-ship* thing big."

Lou agreed, but Willow's words settled on her like a lead vest. It was easy to forget her problems with the murder and Kimberly's sketchy behavior at times like this, when she was having fun with her best friend and planning for the future.

As much as Lou loved the idea of sprucing up the book-store and getting the town behind her, she worried it might not be enough to change the image of Button Books, especially if Frederick's murderer was still out there, possibly plotting to kill again.

CHAPTER 18

Lou spent the next day executing the plan she and Willow had laid out the night before. After a cozy morning with the cats and a cup of coffee, she started with a trip to the bakery.

Button Bakery was adjacent from the bookshop, on the other side of Thimble Drive. It was a gloomy January day, and foggy clouds sat low around the town, so thick that they almost looked like snow suspended around the eves of the buildings downtown. Lou pulled her knit cap lower around her ears as she jogged across the street.

Entering the bakery was like walking into a ray of sunshine. The place immediately warmed her up and brightened her day. The air sparkled with the sweet scent of sugar, and the comforting smells of baking swirled around Lou, dragging her farther inside.

"Welcome to the Button Bakery. What can I help you with today?" asked a woman around Lou's age, with blonde hair pulled back into a French braid.

"I'm Lou, from the bookstore." Lou stepped forward, motioning across the intersection before holding out her hand.

The woman's eyes lit up, but Lou couldn't quite read the emotion behind the reaction. Was the woman curious? Happy? Lou hoped for the latter.

"Lindsey," the woman said, shaking Lou's hand. "So nice to meet you. What can I get for you?" She glanced over at the bakery cases full of cupcakes, delicious-looking cakes, tarts, and every other confectionary creation Lou could've dreamed of.

"I need to try a slice of that coconut rum cake." Lou pointed at the dessert case to the lightest, fluffiest white cake she'd ever seen, topped with a white frosting and coated with coconut. "But I'm actually here to order something for the reopening celebration I'm going to be holding for the bookstore next week."

Lindsey grabbed a notepad from behind the register and flipped it open to a new page. "What were you thinking?"

Lou couldn't help but beam as she explained her idea. "I hope a week is enough notice, because I was hoping for February eleventh."

She had a really cute idea for a *falling in love with a story* display for Valentines Day and felt like a little over a week would give her enough time to get the last-minute touches ready.

When Lindsey nodded that the timing was okay with her, Lou continued. "I was thinking cupcakes, but I'm open to other ideas. Just something we could serve customers on the first night."

"Cupcakes are a great idea." Lindsey jotted down notes. "Any ideas on flavors?"

"I'm open." Lou shrugged. "Any suggestions?"

"Our Boston cream cupcakes are some of our best sellers. We could try those." Lindsey inhaled sharply as if she'd just gotten a great idea. "Oh, and what if I make a little cookie book to sit on top of each one?"

The baker's enthusiasm was contagious. "That sounds amazing," Lou said, then paused. "But do you think you could fit a book and a cat on each one?"

Lindsey cocked an eyebrow at Lou, showing she needed more explanation.

"I'm going to be rebranding the bookshop slightly. I've recently accumulated quite a few foster cats, and I'm thinking of running the bookshop as a cat rescue center as well. People can shop for books, but they can also spend time with adoptable cats." It was the first time Lou had explained the concept to anyone other than Willow or Noah. She curled her fingers into her palms, hoping it didn't sound crazy.

From the warm smile that spread over Lindsey's face, Lou had her answer. "That sounds wonderful," Lindsey said, taking more notes. "And, yes, I can definitely add a book and a cat to the top of each cupcake."

Lou paid the deposit on the order, and Lindsey shook her hand once more. "This is such a fun idea," she said. "I'm glad the bookstore will be in good hands again."

"Right." Lou hadn't missed Lindsey's dig at Kimberly. "Speaking of the former owner, you haven't seen her around, have you?" Lou asked since the bakery had been closed when Lou and Willow had done their initial search the other day.

"I'm sorry. I haven't. I'll keep my eyes open, though. Did you need anything else?" Lindsey asked when Lou lingered at the counter.

"I wasn't kidding about that coconut rum slice. I'd really love to try it," Lou said sheepishly.

Laughing, Lindsey shook her head. "Oh, I totally forgot. Yes, let me get you a piece to go." She cut a slice and packed it up for Lou, saying it was on the house since she got distracted.

Lou thanked her and clutched her confectionary treasure as she walked out onto the foggy streets. After dropping off the slice of cake at home, Lou went about her other errands.

She wandered around the Antique Button for far too long, getting distracted by all the wonderful pieces they had. But her meandering paid off because she found a few gorgeous rugs tucked away in a corner. Along with the three lamps she bought there, it was too much to carry.

"I can load it into my truck and swing it by later today, if that's okay," said the owner, who insisted Lou call him Smitty.

"That would be wonderful," Lou said, squeezing his hand tight as they shook on the deal. It helped ease her guilt that she was close, so it wouldn't be a long trip for the man to drop off her items.

In the same fashion, she arranged for the Bean and Button to supply hot coffee, tea, and cocoa for opening night. She bought some cozy throw blankets that doubled as shawls from Button Boutique—as well as a couple new outfits for herself—and picked up some new toys, scratching posts, and treats for the cats from the local pet store. She inquired about Kimberly again at each place but was met with the same blank stares and shaking heads.

Her last stop of the day was The Upholstered Button. She trotted across the roundabout in the center of downtown and slipped inside the furniture store. Inside smelled like Material Girls had, with that clean fabric scent, but with the added richness of stained wood.

The furniture was gorgeous, and Lou's focus snagged on a few pieces she wanted for her apartment upstairs. But before she could sit on a chair or run her fingers along a sofa table, a woman came sauntering over to her. She was clearly in her fifties or older and had her sleek gray hair twisted up into a decorative clip at the nape of her neck. She wore flowing, silky fabrics that mirrored the gliding way she moved. A pashmina scarf had been tossed over one of her shoulders, completing her comfortable yet classy look.

"You're from the bookstore." The gray-haired woman narrowed her eyes at Lou but not in a judging way. It was more of a mind-reading way. She gasped. "And you're here to get some new furniture for the shop." The statement held the same tone as *thank goodness,* telling Lou she wasn't the only one who'd noticed the threadbare pieces and their need for a new home.

"How did you know all that?" Lou leaned in close, wondering if she was in the presence of an actual psychic.

The woman's face broke into a wide grin, making her immediately more approachable. "My son is one of Willow's students. She warned me you'd be coming by. Described you perfectly. I'm Beatrice, but you can call me Bea." The woman winked at Lou and waved for her to follow as she led the way to a living-room set.

Bea had done a lot of thinking about what pieces should go in the bookshop. Willow had even warned her about the cats. She'd researched fabrics that would be easy to clean, that wouldn't attract too much fur, and she even looked into ordering special cat scratchers that would slip under each foot of the chairs to protect their edges from claws.

As it turned out, the only thing Bea couldn't help with was locating Kimberly. "I'm not sad she's gone, I have to admit. That one was always in some trouble or another."

Lou was on her way back to the bookshop, an order slip

with a delivery date for her new furniture clutched in her hand, when she spotted Noah up ahead, standing in front of the candy shop.

He waved. "You seem like you're in a good mood," he said. "Glad to see all those cats aren't gettin' you down."

She laughed. "They're great. I've just been getting things ready for the reopening and I'm having fun."

As they talked, a girl ran out of the candy shop and stood shyly behind Noah. Lou instantly knew she had to be his daughter. She had the same dark eyes and almost black hair, not to mention the adorable dimples in each cheek, just like her dad.

"Lou, I'd like you to meet my daughter, Marigold." Noah gestured to the girl who clutched a bag of chocolate-covered gummy worms.

Lou smiled. So this was the Marigold she'd heard Easton and Noah discussing before. "It's nice to meet you."

The girl appeared to be elementary school aged—maybe third or fourth grade, Lou guessed. She handed her dad the bag of sweets and held out her hand. "Hello."

Lou's heart just about melted at the girl's great manners. She had the same confidence about her that her dad exuded.

"Goldie, this is the woman I was telling you about, the new owner of the bookshop." Noah placed a hand on his daughter's shoulder.

The girl's eyes crinkled in the corners just like her dad's when she smiled big.

"Marigold loves to read," Noah explained.

"Me too." Lou put her hands on her knees so she was closer to Marigold's height. "What's your favorite book right now?"

The *right now* was an important qualifier all readers understand. The idea of *one favorite book* was often too weighty a decision to be made. Plus, true readers know favorites change with seasons and moods. Lou had a favorite book for when she was happy, one she loved to read when the weather was warm, and another she pulled out if it was pouring rain or if she was feeling sad.

Marigold wet her lips and smiled. "I'm really into the Warriors series right now."

Lou's eyes widened at the girl's mention of the fantasy series that followed clans of forest cats. "The Warriors books are great. I just ordered the full set for the bookstore. So you like cats, then?" Lou's gaze flicked up to meet Noah's.

"I already mentioned to her how you're going to run adoptions as well as selling books." Noah's tone was warm as he looked down at his daughter. "Marigold loves cats, but her mom is allergic."

Marigold grabbed on to her dad's jacket again. "But now that Mom has her own house, maybe we could get a cat at your place?"

Noah laughed. "We'll see, petal." He patted her back.

Noticing the redness flooding Noah's cheeks at his daughter's mention of her parents' separate houses, Lou jumped in, "You're always welcome at the bookshop, Marigold, even before I'm officially open. These cats need a lot of love and attention. I'm sure they'd love to have you come and hang out with them, anytime."

The girl's face lit up. She checked with her dad for confirmation. Noah grinned. "That sounds like a great compromise. Speaking of your mom, here she is." Noah looked past Lou and handed the bag of candy back to Marigold.

Turning around, Lou noticed someone she'd met before, albeit over video.

"Cassidy?" Lou asked as the real estate agent who'd helped her purchase the bookshop walked up.

Cassidy's smile widened as she recognized Lou. She flung her arms wide and pulled her into a hug. "Oh, it's so great to meet you in person." She squeezed tight.

"You too." Lou stepped back.

Cassidy was flawlessly put together, just as she'd always appeared on the video calls they'd had. Her blonde hair fell in a shiny curtain down her back. She wore a smart black wool coat over what looked like a skirt suit, the outfit completed with patent-red heels. "I meant to stop by earlier to say hello, but I've been dealing with a nightmare client." Cassidy sucked in a breath through clenched teeth.

Lou waved a hand. "No worries. You did me a huge favor by meeting the movers."

Glancing at her daughter, Cassidy held out her hand. Marigold ran over, and her mother pulled her into a hug. "Good to see you, pumpkin. Did you meet Lou?"

Marigold nodded. She opened the bag of chocolates and chewed one in half.

"Glad to see Dad's not worried about ruining your dinner." Cassidy laughed and looked at Noah.

Lou did too, wondering if she was witnessing a passive-aggressive exchange, but Noah's eyes sparkled. "Nice try. You've got hours to do that yourself."

In response, Cassidy dug into the candy bag and plucked out a chocolate-covered gummy worm, biting it in half just like her daughter. "Okay, kid. Let's get you home. Thanks, Noah. Thursday still works for you?"

He nodded and gave Marigold a salute, which the girl returned.

"Nice to meet you, Miss Lou." Marigold turned around

and waved as they walked past. "Mom, how strong is your cat allergy?" the little girl asked as they walked away.

Noah and Lou shared a chuckle before they parted ways too. Lou headed for the bookshop, feeling better than she had in a long time. Today had felt so perfect, being able to focus on her shop and her new hometown. Maybe she needed to put Frederick's death behind her. The constant sneaking around and investigating potential suspects was obviously having a negative effect on her. Easton was a good detective. He would figure out the truth, if he hadn't already. She'd left him a note with the key and her suspicions. That had to be enough.

A sense of peace fell over Lou as she thought about letting go of the investigation. That good feeling sank to the icy ground as she stopped at the bookshop. In her absence, someone had painted a message onto the cold glass.

Don't trust this shop!

Lime-green paint dripped down the windows of the front door, pooling on the wood muntins. Was this the work of the same person who left the threatening message on the answering machine or someone different?

Lou glanced over her shoulder, opened the door, and went inside to grab cleaning supplies. The painted words might wash away from the door, but they felt stained in her brain, reminding her what was at stake.

CHAPTER 19

L ou's satisfying, yet brief, decision to take a step back and leave the investigation alone had to be reevaluated after the shop door was vandalized.

"It's obvious you can't leave this alone," Willow said that afternoon when she stopped by after work.

Lou had explained everything to her about her day, her decision to let Easton handle the investigation, and the threatening message. Willow paced, stepping over sleeping cats with each pass.

Lou made a mental note to make signs for the front door to warn customers to watch their step. It was just one more item to add to her to-do list. After a day that had made her feel so ready to open, those painted words had brought everything to a crashing halt.

"The new signage should be ready next week." Lou ran a hand over Sapphire's soft fur. He was curled up in her lap under the table. "That should help people know that the shop is under new management." But even as Lou said it, she knew it might not make the difference she'd hoped. She'd changed her outgoing message on the phone and this had still happened.

Willow snapped her fingers. "We need to talk to that Eloise character like we planned yester—argh." She stumbled forward in surprise as Romeow jumped onto her head from the top of a bookshelf.

Lou raced to help. "Romeow," she scolded as she tried to pry the kitten from her friend's head, careful to not intensify the scratches Willow had undoubtedly already received. "I'm so sorry," Lou told Willow with an exasperated eye roll. "This is his newest trick. It's not enough that he destroys books. Now he's trying to scratch me up anytime I walk close enough for him to tackle me. I didn't see him behind you until it was too late."

Willow tapped at her cheek to see if one of the bigger scratches was bleeding. When her fingers came away clean, she said, "No worries. I was more surprised than anything." She laughed now that any sense of danger had worn off. "You're quite the troublemaker, aren't you?" She pointed an accusatory finger at the kitten.

Lou placed him on the floor as Willow moved away from the bookshelves.

"Easton isn't back yet?" Lou asked. Did they really want to go talk with a potential murderer on their own?

Willow shrugged and sat across from Lou at the table. "Not as of this morning, but I left pretty early. Plus, you said yourself that he thinks it was the loan sharks. He won't do anything about an old lady." She stood again and stepped over The Great Catsby, who hadn't caused a single furniture-scratching incident since Lou had given him those two spray bottle warnings.

"And what are *we* going to do?" Lou asked quietly.

Pausing with her constant movement, Willow chewed at her lip as she contemplated that. "We can at least see if she has an alibi. If she does, we'll leave it alone and figure out a different way to tackle the bad press for the bookshop."

"I think a better use of our time is to find Kimberly. That guy I told you about, Quinn, he said he hasn't seen her in a couple of days. He seemed worried." Lou scratched at Sapphy's ears. "He also mentioned that she was hanging out in Kirk a lot more since she sold the shop. He gave me a list of her favorite places." Lou pulled up the list she'd added to the notes on her phone and showed Willow.

She scanned the list. "I know where most of those places are." Her tone dropped at the end, not sounding one bit excited. When Lou shot her a questioning look, Willow said, "It would've been kinda cool to corner a killer and have her confess."

Lou shivered. "I think that sounds terrifying. Cornering a killer would mean that we were then in a room with someone who'd murdered another person and might kill us to keep it a secret."

Willow's shoulders sank a few inches. "Yeah, I guess."

"I'll tell you what. If you can convince Easton to come with us, I'll go talk to Eloise," Lou said in compromise.

"Really?" Willow's face brightened, but her smile immediately dropped. "I'd say yes, but I think you'll have a better chance of getting him to help. He seems to like you, whereas me …"

Lou had to admit Easton acted differently around her than he did with Willow, but she had a gut feeling that he liked Willow just as much. Some people just have too much fun being enemies.

"Okay, should I call him, or should we see if he's home?" Lou asked.

Biting her lip for a moment, Willow said, "Let's see if he's home, first. It'll just take us a short drive to check. Plus, I should feed OC and Steve if we're going to head out to Kirk for the evening."

Easton's car wasn't in his driveway when they pulled up to the house. Willow disappeared out back to feed the animals, but Lou stayed out front to make the call.

"Hello," the detective answered on the first ring. "Everything okay, Lou?"

She wobbled her head. "Uh, sort of. Where are you right now?"

"At the station," he answered. "I was just reading over the note you left, actually. Sorry, I was off for a couple days, but I still can't say this makes much of a difference."

Lou squeezed her eyes shut, willing him to be open-minded. "I really think it does, Easton. First editions can sell for a lot of money, and if the people Frederick sold them to found out they were faked, they would be out of a ton of cash, not to mention embarrassed that they fell for a scam. I'm not sure how Kimberly was involved, but my shop's bookmarks were in the fake first editions. Besides the angry voice-mail, my front door was vandalized as well. I'm not saying it's the killer, but I just think this is something we should look into."

"We?" Easton asked, a grin coating his voice.

She pursed her lips. "Here's the thing. I know you talked with that Lance guy from the used bookstore in Silver Lake. But there's another used bookdealer in the county and she's shady. Lance told us he wouldn't be surprised if she was the one who killed Frederick."

Easton stayed silent for a moment. "Okay. I'll go talk to her with you."

"And Willow," Lou added quickly.

Silence stretched out on the other end of the line for longer than Lou felt comfortable with. She opened her mouth to speak several times, but he finally said, "Fine. You want me to come pick you two up?"

"Sure," Lou said. "We're at Willow's."

"See you soon." He hung up just as Willow walked around the house, picking a piece of hay off her jeans.

She glanced at the neighboring house. "Still no Easton? Darn. Looks like we're on our own." Willow wore a triumphant smirk.

Lou smirked right back. "Actually, he's going to take us. He's on his way now."

Willow groaned and then said, "You must really be magical. Convincing Easton to drive out to Kirk just to question an old lady can't have been an easy feat."

"I may have left out the old lady part." Lou grimaced. "And I think you should too. We'll spend the ride there convincing him of her ability to do this, and he won't be able to say no by the time we reach her shop."

Willow laughed just as Easton's car pulled up the driveway. "I think I'm rubbing off on you."

They climbed into Easton's car, Lou in the passenger seat and Willow in the back. Easton's car was warm, and Lou appreciated the heater going full blast given the cold day they were having.

"Okay, where are we going?" Easton asked as he backed up toward his house and then headed down the driveway. He stopped at the end of their shared driveway when neither of the women answered.

"The thing is …" Lou started, but lost her nerve. She folded her hands in her lap and glanced out the window.

"There are a few things you need to know first," Willow finished for her. "The first being that we've been to Frederick's apartment."

Easton whirled around in his seat so he could see Willow. "What?"

Lou wrinkled her nose. "The key I left you, the one I found at the bookshop, well, it opened a secret safe at Frederick's place."

"We searched that whole place. I didn't see any …" His words faded away.

"Any secret safes hidden in the wall?" Willow asked pointedly. "Of course, because you didn't have this one with you." She motioned to Lou. "The woman notices details no one else does."

Easton scowled at Willow but then turned to Lou. "How did you get inside?" Easton asked.

Lou watched him, hoping he wouldn't be mad that she'd broken in. "I knew he liked Vonnegut, so I tried the title of one of his short stories and it worked." She decided not to tell him about the many other tries before that.

He blinked, looking from Lou back to Willow.

"Again, I told you she's detail oriented," Willow said, as if that should've answered all of his questions.

"Inside the safe, which the key opens, I found a threatening letter from the woman we need to go question." Lou wiggled her toes in her boots, eager to get on the road. She wasn't sure what time Eloise's shop closed, but they were losing precious time talking.

Easton pinched at the bridge of his nose. "Okay, let me get

this straight. You broke into a murder victim's home and stole—"

Lou held up a finger. "I didn't take anything. I put it all back and then left the key with you."

"A person who assumed the case was solved," Willow pointed out. "Loan sharks do not kill people, Easton," she scoffed.

Easton sighed like he needed another vacation at that moment. He took a few seconds, his eyes flicking around as if he were trying to get his scattered thoughts in order. "What did this note say?"

Lou sat up straight. "Uh, she said she knew what he'd done, and she wouldn't let him get away with it. She also said something about being two steps ahead of him until the day he died."

Finally, Easton said, "Okay, tell me where I'm going."

Willow and Lou shared a look of triumph before Willow leaned forward and gave Easton directions. On the way there, Lou recounted what Lance Swatek had reported about Eloise, how she found older, rich collectors and pretended to befriend them so she could get an early shot at their estate sales when they passed away.

"You think she might have something to do with their deaths?" Easton asked as they pulled into Kirk.

"Lance sure seemed to," Willow said.

Easton drove in silence for the next few minutes as he navigated through the crowded streets of Kirk. Lou could see how the bustling city could be seen as a metropolis to residents of Button. After years living in New York, Lou knew her standards were different. Easton took a turn into the old-town portion of the city. Here the storefronts were smaller and looked as if they'd been there a lot longer. They stopped in front of one that held a sign that read Pages Books.

Willow and Lou unbuckled their seat belts, but Easton held out a hand to stop them. "Oh no. You two are staying here. I'm going to question her myself."

"Come on." Willow's tone was tight with exasperation. "You wouldn't even have this lead if it weren't for Lou."

"What if we come in after you and pretend to be shopping for books?" Lou asked. "We just want to listen. We don't need to ask her any of the questions. We'll leave that to you."

Easton thought for a moment. "Okay, a couple minutes behind me." He tossed Lou the keys and said, "Lock up when you leave."

Willow let out a celebratory whoop, and Lou clutched the keys tight in her hand. They watched Easton walk into the building and then got out of the car. Walking down the street a little, they tried to make it seem like they had just been passing by, instead of deliberately coming to this shop.

A bell rang at the front door. "Welcome," called the old woman Lou had spoken to at the book swap. She hoped Eloise wouldn't recognize her. "Let me know if you need anything."

"Thanks, we're just browsing," Willow said, catching Lou's cautious body language.

They pretended to scan the books on a low table in the corner while Easton started in with his questioning.

"I'm sorry. I just have a few questions for you about Frederick Alvarado. Did you know him well?" Easton asked.

Eloise snorted. "I thought I did, but apparently he's out there pawning fakes. He was already a thorn in my side because he kept beating me to a lot of the stock in the area, but now I have actual cause to hate the man."

Lou winced. Eloise was speaking in the present tense about

174

Frederick. Either it was an act, or she didn't know the man was dead.

"Mrs. Huff, we found Frederick dead last Saturday. We're treating his death as a homicide. Where were you on the night of Friday the twenty-first?"

Eloise coughed. "Dead? Homicide?" Lou glanced over her shoulder to see the older woman fanning herself with a nearby book. "I haven't ... I didn't ... I was with my daughter."

Easton clicked open a pen and pulled out a notebook. "Can I get her name and number?"

Swallowing, Eloise nodded. She gave Easton the information. "Two of her coworkers were with us. We had dinner at her house," she added, continuing to fan herself. But after a second, she stopped. "Wait, you think I might've had something to do with this? That's why you're asking where I was when he died." It was as if she were just putting it together.

"We're just questioning anyone with motive, ma'am." Easton leveled her with a serious stare. "And we found a threatening letter you wrote him."

Eloise's face flushed. "Oh, that." She laughed nervously. "Well, that was something I wrote in the heat of the moment. I'd only just learned of the scam he was trying to pull over on his customers, my customers. The used-book business is small, so we have a lot of the same buyers."

"Can I get the names of the buyers who informed you of the fake first editions?" Easton asked, jotting down their names and numbers as well. When he was done, he tipped his head forward. "Thank you for your time. I'll be in touch after I check into your alibi."

And with that, he left, not even making eye contact with Lou or Willow. He was good.

It took Eloise a moment to collect herself before she came over to the women. "Seeing anything you like?" she asked.

Lou ended up buying a set of the Seekers series by Erin Hunter, the author of the Warriors series, Noah's daughter liked. If Marigold loved the author's first series, she might be interested in trying another.

Eloise might be a terrible person, but she most likely hadn't been the one to kill Frederick.

CHAPTER 20

After exiting Eloise's used bookshop, Lou and Willow walked down the street a few hundred feet before turning around and heading back to Easton's car. He waited outside, recording voice notes on his phone. Lou remembered they had his keys. He glanced up as Lou threw him his keys, and they all bustled inside.

"You were right, Lou. I think we might be onto something here. I'm going to investigate these buyers. If some of them are mad enough that they're leaving you threatening messages, they might've tried to confront Frederick about it."

"Another person who might have some good information is Kimberly Collins," Willow said from the back seat. The lightness in Willow's tone told Lou that she was trying to be nonchalant about what she was asking. Maybe because Easton could help them find Kimberly too.

Lou nodded. "She's been missing for a few days. I've been worried that she might be in trouble too. If she was involved with this first-edition scam with Frederick, the same person who came after him might've come for her too."

Easton's eyebrows rose. "Good thought." He pulled out his laptop from his messenger bag stashed behind the front seat and started typing. "Let me pull up the address we have on file for her." He clenched his jaw as his eyes moved down the screen. "It's your address." He motioned to Lou.

Lou pulled out her phone. "I have a list of places she might be around here from her sort-of boyfriend."

"Sort of?" Easton asked.

"Long story. No time," Willow said, shoving the phone toward Easton. "Let's hit these spots."

By the time the sun had set, they'd visited the two bars, the salon, her favorite restaurant, and the shoe store. Kimberly wasn't at any of them, nor had the people working seen any sign of her in the last few days. *It was helpful to have a cop along*, Lou realized. The few times they'd hit resistance, Easton merely had to take out his badge, and the information flowed. That badge was like Drano for answers.

The next place on the list was the thrift store called By a Thread in the trendy downtown area of Kirk. Easton peered at the screen of Lou's phone as she showed him the address.

"It's after seven. A thrift store won't be open this late," he said.

"Says it's open until midnight." Willow pointed to the hours listed on the screen and the green *Open now* letters under the business name.

"It seems like a pretty bougie place," Lou observed, flicking through the pictures on the site. "Maybe they've found that people who want to buy two-hundred-dollar, used snakeskin boots shop at night." She shrugged.

"Okay." Easton started the ignition. "I might drop the two of you off at this one and jog over to Frederick's apartment in

Tinsdale, if you don't mind. I'd like to look at this safe and its contents myself."

"Sure." Lou clicked her seat belt into place.

"And if there's no Kimberly in sight, we can shop until you get back." Willow smiled.

Easton drove to By a Thread while Lou described the steps he would need to take to locate the hidden compartment in Frederick's wall. Once she was done explaining, Easton patted his jacket pocket, showing he'd brought the key along with him.

He dropped them off in front of the thrift store with directions to call if they needed him, but he would be quick.

Willow and Lou headed inside. By a Thread was open, but it was difficult to tell at first glance. The lighting was dim, and they didn't post the hours on the door like most businesses. There was a bell to let the guy behind the counter know customers had entered, and the man's eyes followed them as they wandered inside.

He didn't call out a welcome or even a hello. He just stood there looking large and angry. Willow widened her eyes at Lou, and they started milling about the racks of clothes.

The store smelled different from what Lou had expected of a thrift store. Others she'd visited over the years seemed to either have a weird musty smell that came from items of varying levels of cleanliness coming from so many previous homes, or they overwhelmingly stank of whatever detergent or spray the clothing had been doused in upon arrival. By a Thread smelled more like expensive leather and the sharp, spicy scent of expensive cologne instead of old fabric.

Checking the prices on a few of the items, Lou realized why. This place was definitely meant for high-end clientele.

The clothing was nice, if not a little quirky for Lou's tastes, but the price tags reflected the brands and quality of each piece.

"This is more than I pay for new clothes," Willow whispered, monitoring the angry gentleman behind the counter.

Lou snorted. Willow shopped at outdoor clothing companies almost exclusively. Even during her day job as a teacher, she was outside most of the time digging around in the dirt and needed clothing that kept her warm and handled the elements well.

Living in New York and working at a major publishing house, Lou had a very different idea of work wear. She'd dressed in suits, dresses, and designer shoes for as long as she could remember. Now that she owned and ran a bookshop, she knew her dress code would lean more toward fluffier, cozier pieces of clothing, none of which she saw on the racks here.

But they weren't really there to shop. Lou scanned the place, noting the handful of other shoppers inside with them. There was a man and woman shopping together, a well-dressed older woman shopping by herself, and a pair of men looking at the shoe section together.

No Kimberly.

"Should we check the fitting rooms?" Lou asked, selecting a cute black dress in her size from the rack in front of her. She gestured toward the set of three changing rooms, eyeing the one in the middle that was in use.

Willow's lips pinched together. "To be honest, this doesn't really seem like the kind of place where Kimberly would shop. Her style was a lot … louder?"

"Still …" Lou held up the dress. Trying it on would give them a reason to hang out by the dressing rooms without seeming suspicious. "I think we should check."

"Okay. I'll wait outside the dressing rooms while you change, to see if anyone comes out," Willow said, leading the way to the other side of the shop where three changing stalls had been constructed from drapery material.

Lou enclosed herself in the changing room on the left. She undressed, her teeth chattering a bit as she took off her warm sweater and pulled on the sleeveless dress. She heard quiet shuffling as the person next to her moved around in the middle changing room. Someone giggled. Lou stopped but shrugged. Maybe they'd chosen something that really didn't fit right. She'd definitely had one of those moments in a dressing room where she just had to laugh at how poorly something fit. But as Lou adjusted the black dress, she saw this garment wasn't one of those. The dress was really nice, actually. She swung back the curtain and posed for Willow.

"Oh, very cute. Look what I found." Willow was bent over, pulling on tall boots. Her own shoes were discarded next to her on the floor. Willow staggered closer as she laced up the second boot. "These are really expensive riding boots. I've been eyeing a pair for years," she whispered, as if the man behind the counter might up the price if he knew what they were really worth.

Lou smiled. "They're very nice. What are they doing in a vintage clothing boutique?"

"I think some people try to wear them as regular old everyday boots," Willow said with a snort. "And even though they're expensive for day-to-day shoes, they're really afford-able for riding boots. Which is what they're meant for."

"And they're your size. Score." Lou pointed to how well the boots fit her friend.

"Double score," Willow pointed to the cute black dress.

"I already have something like this in my closet." Lou shook her head. "But you should definitely get those boots."

Lou had donated many of her day-to-day outfits, knowing she wouldn't need multiple suits or dry-clean-only skirt and sweater sets in Button. She'd kept her favorites along with a couple of nicer dresses she'd used for parties in the city, but other than that, she had little use for those kinds of outfits anymore.

She was about to return to the dressing room to change back into her clothes when she motioned toward the middle stall in question. Willow surreptitiously shook her head to show no one had come out while Lou had been changing.

That was odd. The middle stall had also been occupied when they'd first arrived. Was the same person still inside? A quick scan of the shop revealed that the man and woman who'd been shopping earlier were nowhere to be seen. Lou hadn't heard the bell ring on the front door. She glanced toward the back corner at the customer bathroom, but the door was open and the light off.

"Did you leave the area at all?" Lou asked.

Willow scratched at her cheek guiltily for a moment. "I mean, I wandered over to the shoes. That's how I found the boots." Willow pointed about ten feet to her left, where a few shelves made up a small shoe section. Her back might've been to the middle stall for a few moments. That didn't seem like long enough for one customer to leave and another to enter.

"Okay." Lou grabbed at the curtain again and was about to pull it back.

"I'm going to buy these while you change." Willow pulled off the boots and slipped back into her own shoes. "If you're not going to get that." She gestured to the dress Lou wore.

Lou shook her head, a frown of confusion on her face as

she contemplated where the couple might've gone. Willow didn't seem to notice her thoughts were elsewhere and rushed off to the register, too excited about purchasing her boots.

Back behind the curtain in the dressing room, Lou slipped out of the dress and pulled on her jeans and sweater. She held her ear close to the middle piece of fabric, trying to hear any other noises within the changing room next to her. It was silent.

Placing the dress back on the hanger, Lou checked to make sure she had everything she came in with, and walked out. The middle curtain was still drawn. Willow's boots sat on the counter, and the sales clerk was opening a bag to put them in as he handed her a receipt. Lou returned the dress to the correct rack and then walked by the changing rooms again. The woman was still shopping alone, but the two men had gone. Again, Lou hadn't heard the bell on the door ring.

Something was up, and she would bet anything it had to do with that middle changing room.

Pretending to examine the items on the rack closest to the changing rooms, Lou peeked into the open room on the right, the one she hadn't used. It appeared identical to the one she'd changed in, with a chair and a standing mirror in the back two corners.

Willow came over, a large bag swinging by her side. "Should I let Easton know we're ready to be picked up?" she asked, pulling out her phone. "I texted him that Kimberly wasn't here while you were changing, but I also told him we were having fun shopping so he shouldn't rush."

"Good." Lou leaned in close to her friend. "I think there's something weird going on." Lou glanced at the man behind the counter.

"Like what?" Willow scoffed.

"The two men, and the man and woman who were in here when we first arrived are gone, but did you hear them leave through the front door, with the bell?" Lou whispered.

Willow frowned. "Maybe we just didn't notice because we were focused on other things. Background noise, you know."

"I heard sounds, giggling when I was in there, but you said no one came out or went in." Lou pointed to the closed drape hanging over the middle changing room. Then, without thinking too much about it, she grabbed Willow's hand and pulled her toward the curtain.

With one last check to make sure the man behind the counter was looking a different way and the woman shopping had her back to them, she flipped open the curtain.

Inside was empty. She pulled Willow in behind her.

"What are you doing?" Willow hissed as she tumbled forward.

Lou closed the curtain behind them and inspected the space. Inside was a mirror and a chair, just like the other two changing rooms. Lou narrowed her eyes.

Wait. Not just like the other two.

This changing room had a full-length mirror hanging on the wall instead of a standing one. Lou studied the mirror, placing her finger onto the surface.

A gap showed up between her fingertip and its reflection, so it wasn't a two-way mirror. Thank goodness. That would've been creepy.

But when Lou took her finger away, the mirror moved. It bounced toward her a few centimeters. She glanced at the edge and pulled.

The mirror swung easily away from the wall. In the space behind it was a hole in the wall that led to a person-sized passageway. Lou beamed back at Willow and then climbed through.

Willow followed. There was a handle on the back of the mirror to pull it closed behind them. They did so and then followed arrows down the hallway to the right. The walls were painted a deep-maroon color and smelled of fresh paint. The carpet also felt new, its thick pile adding cushion underfoot as they navigated down the long hallway. Then, after about a hundred feet, they came upon a sign on the wall.

The Vault.

Next to the sign was a large wooden door with a metal snake handle. They opened the door warily.

Inside was a dimly lit tavern. A large wooden bar sat in one corner. The bartenders wore white button-up shirts and black half aprons. About twenty small tables took up the rest of the space.

Willow and Lou shared a look of surprise. They'd found a speakeasy.

They knew all about these. During Willow's last visit to New York a couple of years ago, they'd made it their mission to find as many as possible using clues from forums on the internet. Even though they weren't illegal anymore, it was fun to follow clues and find the secret bars.

Willow inhaled and motioned with a slight jerk of her head toward a table in the center of the room. She whispered, "Kimberly."

They'd found her.

CHAPTER 21

The bartender of the secret bar evaluated them with interest. "What can I get for you two?" he asked while polishing a glass.

Lou wondered if he really had to hand wash all the glasses or if he just kept one at the bar to polish from time to time to add to the atmosphere.

"I'll take a French Seventy-Five, please," Lou said.

"Sazerac for me." Willow held up a finger.

He started on their drinks, but Lou couldn't help but feel like she'd seen him before.

"Your bookstore open yet?" he asked with a half smile, noticing her studying him.

She snapped her fingers. "You were the one who stopped by looking for used books the other day." Lou's brain let out an *I told you so* tingle. She'd seen a few Bradbury and Salinger titles in the used-book section when she was organizing. She would have to put those aside for him to look through. "Next week," she said, giving him the date and time for her reopening celebration.

"I'll be sure to stop by," he said, handing over their drinks.

Once they'd paid, they took their drinks over to an empty table close to where Kimberly sat. She was with another woman, and they were laughing hysterically about something. From their wobbly postures, Lou wondered if it was really that funny or if they'd just over-imbibed.

Lou scanned the place and noticed both the couple and the two men who'd been shopping in the vintage clothing store when they'd entered were now seated in the bar, sipping at cocktails.

Willow placed her large shopping bag on the floor next to her. She sipped at her drink. "The man knows his stuff." She held up her drink and gave the bartender a nod of approval.

Lou tasted her French 75 and smiled.

Willow pulled out her phone. "Should I text Easton?" she whispered. "It's funny, I feel like I shouldn't bring a cop to a speakeasy, but I keep forgetting it's not illegal."

Lou shook her head. "Actually, I think it's good he's not here. Kimberly would recognize him, right?"

Willow touched the tip of her nose. "Oh, good thinking."

"And I'm guessing, based on the trouble she's gotten into, that she won't be as open to talking around a detective as she would be around the two of us." Lou played with the lemon peel twist hanging on the rim of her drink.

"Then it's up to us to get the information out of her." Willow winked and stood, taking her drink and her bag with her over to where Kimberly sat. Lou followed with her drink.

The table Kimberly and her friend occupied was a four-seater. Lou and Willow slid into the empty seats. Kimberly and the other woman she was with were in another fit of giggles, but the laughter quickly died down as they noticed the two intruders.

"Hey, we're sitting h—" Kimberly's accusatory question cut short as she noticed Willow. "Wait. I know you."

Willow took a sip of her drink. "We met in Button. This is my friend Lou. She bought the bookstore from you."

At this, Kimberly's wide smile dropped. Or maybe it was because she'd looked at Lou and realized she wasn't smiling or amused.

"You didn't tell me about all the fun voicemails I'd be getting, or the angry messages people would paint on my door." Lou kept her tone sweet, but knew her words were getting through to Kimberly when the woman flinched.

Moving as if to leave, Kim froze when Willow said, "Not so fast," under her breath. She moved her phone to the table and added, "I've got a police officer waiting outside. He'll be in here in a split second if you try to move."

Kimberly settled back into her seat. But her friend, who had sobered up quickly at Willow's mention of the cops, stood and said, "You're on your own with this, Kimmie. Call me later." She turned on her heel and left. Kimberly scowled at her friend's back and sniffed like she was contemplating throwing a fit.

Lou studied the woman who used to own her bookshop. She appeared to be in her late thirties, like Willow and Lou. But unlike them, she seemed lost. Thinking back to her first encounter with George, Lou felt the opposite sensation after meeting this woman. Kimberly might be about twice George's age, but it was clear to Lou that Kimberly didn't know what she wanted out of life or who she wanted to be.

"Fine, what do you want?" Kimberly crossed her arms with a pout.

Lou scoffed, "To know why you were selling fake first editions." Lou kept her voice down as she noticed they'd attracted the attention of the surrounding tables. Once the other patrons return to their conversations, Lou added, "We saw the bookmarks inside."

But Lou needn't have whispered because Kimberly blurted out, "It was Frederick." Her statement was loud enough that the people at the nearby tables turned to look. "It was his idea to sell them. I found a box of old books my aunt had put aside. I brought them to Frederick, who said most people wouldn't know the difference. He convinced me we could sell them for a huge profit and no one would be the wiser. Well, that was a lie, wasn't it? They obviously found out." Her voice was tight, and it wobbled like a guitar string that had been plucked.

Lou's mouth hung open. Willow's did too.

Before either of them could respond, a man in a booth next to them stood. He wore a beautifully tailored suit, had a gray handlebar mustache and wore a tweed hat.

"Excuse me, but I couldn't help but overhear," he said, addressing Kimberly in the most polite but furious tone Lou had ever experienced. "I need you to know that you are quite mistaken. Frederick Alvarado would never sell anything that wasn't authentic." He sniffed in her direction—the more polite version of spitting at her.

"How would you know?" Kimberly scoffed, rolling her eyes at the man.

"I knew Frederick better than anyone. I was his tailor, after all." The man straightened his tie with pride as he glowered down at Kimberly.

Lou's eyes went wide. The tags in the suit that had been cut out. Was it because the suit had been custom made, and finding this tailor would've led the police straight to a person who would've identified Frederick right away?

"You made his suit?" Lou asked in surprise.

"I did." The tailor nodded. "And I'll tell you young ladies the same thing I was just telling Gerald." He waved a hand over at the bar. "There is no way Frederick was involved in selling fake first editions or anything else he's been accused of. It's bad enough he's dead. Let us not besmirch the man's immaculate name."

His words hit Lou in the chest. They felt right. She'd had a good feeling about Frederick. Even though she'd only inter-acted with him for mere minutes, he hadn't seemed like the kind of person to swindle people with something scammy like poorly faked first editions.

"Well, something's going on because Frederick and Victor are both dead, and someone is obviously mad at you, Kimber-ly." Willow glanced over at the woman, whose eyes had become shifty and her face flushed pink.

"Victor's dead?" Her voice broke around the question and her fingers shook.

Lou swallowed past a lump in her throat, remembering how Quinn said they were an item, at least at one point or another.

Cheeks reddening at her earlier bluntness, Willow said, "The police said it was a hit and run, but he had missing fingers like maybe some loan sharks had paid him a visit."

Kimberly sucked in a startled gasp. "I couldn't find him for a few days. I knew he'd gotten into money trouble, but I figured he'd show back up soon. You don't think the same people who hurt him killed Frederick? Or ..." She flinched as she seemed to remember something. "Oh, Vic. You didn't," she muttered.

"Didn't what?" Lou asked, leaning closer.

The tailor slipped into the vacant chair at the table, inter-ested as well.

Kimberly looked around at all of them before sniffling and saying, "Victor always owed the wrong people money. He would push their deadlines way further than even I was comfortable with. But he would laugh and tell me he had a secret weapon. His brother had a really expensive book. Vic said if he ever got really desperate, he would sell Freddie's book." Kimberly's eyes flicked around the table as if they might know what had happened. "You don't think he sent the loan sharks after Freddie's book and they killed him when he wouldn't give it to them?"

The tailor clicked his tongue. "That must've been his signed first edition of *Slaughterhouse-Five*. He would go on at length about that book. He loved it."

Kimberly snorted. "Oh no. Vic knew better than to touch *that* book. Plus, that one's only worth about a grand. The book he was talking about was a signed first edition of *The Catcher in the Rye* Freddie stumbled upon in a storage container when he was visiting the East Coast last year. Vic priced it out before and thought he could get about sixty grand for it."

"Sixty grand?" Willow wheezed in surprise.

"Vic told me there was something special about the signature. It was the author's childhood nickname or something, so it more than doubled the price they could get for it," Kimberly explained.

Lou sat back, the weight of Kimberly's words feeling like a kick to Lou's gut. She didn't know exactly what happened, but it definitely sounded like a possibility that the loan sharks went after an expensive book. While she'd seen the signed copy of *Slaughterhouse-Five* in Frederick's safe, she hadn't seen *The Catcher in the Rye*.

Willow glanced down at her phone. "Easton's coming our way," she whispered to Lou.

But Kimberly must've heard her because she froze. "You still called the cops on me?" She peered around frantically as if he might already be there. "I stayed. I talked. What more do you want?"

Lou held out a hand. "Whoa, hold on," she said calmly.

"Fine." Kimberly's eyes were wide and wild. "Fine, I'll tell you the truth. Just don't bring the cops into this. He was right." She gestured to the tailor. "It wasn't Freddie. None of it was Freddie. It was me and Vic the whole time."

About to correct her, Lou held her tongue, waiting to see what other information she might spill.

"I found the box of books, like I said before, and I asked Vic to have Freddie inspect them, see if any of them were worth anything in the pile because I had no idea what those kind of things were worth." She shook her head. "Freddie was out of town on some last-minute book-buying expedition, but Vic had been helping him in the shop and knew a few things. He said they were fakes, but only a small number of people could tell if we scuffed up the first edition stamp a little more, so it wasn't obviously different. He was sure we could sell them for a boatload and said he'd split it with me fifty-fifty. We were toying with the idea of doing fake dedication pages too, but that seemed like a harder sell."

Lou thought back to the dedication she knew Olivia Queen hadn't written. She'd been right. It was a fake.

Kimberly shrugged. "After that, I didn't hear from Vic again. I thought he hadn't been able to sell any, but then some guy came into the bookshop all angry with me. He had a fake first edition with the shop bookmark inside. Which meant Vic had swindled me out of my half, and he wouldn't answer my calls. That's when you said your friend might want to buy the shop," Kimberly said, gesturing to Willow. "So I jumped on it.

I needed money too, and I'd been counting on the cash from Victor. Then, last week, I went searching for him. His place was trashed, and there was blood on the carpet. I figured he was in trouble, so I've been hiding out ever since."

The tailor shook his head. "Frederick texted me a few days before he died, saying he was worried his brother was up to something. Victor changed the password on Frederick's email while he was traveling, and he couldn't access his account."

"Frederick must've got back in town, found out that Vic was pawning these books off on his customers and was trying to get to the bottom of what was going on." Lou sat up straight. "That must've been why he came to me, all frantic, looking for you. He couldn't find Victor either and knew you might be the other one who knew something since your book-shop name was on the bookmarks."

Kimberly studied her hands. "I didn't think they would mess with you, honestly," she said, not meeting Lou's eyes. "I thought they would leave you alone once they saw I'd sold the place."

Lou tapped her toe nervously under the table. "But it's not your name on the bookmark, it's the shop name. And since it sounds like someone killed Frederick over the fake first editions, thinking he sold them, my life is in danger too. All because Victor owed the wrong people money."

The back of her neck grew cold. Lou shivered at the reality of her situation.

CHAPTER 22

Kimberly's phone rang, and her expression paled. "Speaking of owing the wrong people money ... I've gotta go." She swigged the rest of her drink and got up.

Lou didn't stop Kimberly. They'd learned all they could from her. Instead, Lou turned to the tailor still sitting with them.

"I'm sorry, we didn't catch your name." She held out her hand.

"Johnathan," he said, taking her hand. "Johnathan Firenze." He flicked a business card out of what seemed like thin air and pushed it toward Lou. "If you ever find yourself in need of a suit, let me know."

Willow's eyes were wide as she observed him, impressed.

"I will." Lou tucked the card into her jacket pocket.

"Heck, I've made half the suits in this room. Oliver, over there." Johnathan waved at a man. "Gerald and Kyle." He waved toward the two bartenders. "Even Tina." He gestured toward a tall woman in a gorgeous gray tweed suit to their left.

"I wish I had known you in my old life," Lou said. "I wore suits every day, just about." She leaned in closer. "What more can you tell us about Frederick?" she asked.

Johnathan sat back. "Now that she mentioned it, I remember Frederick talking about that Salinger first edition. He didn't tell me the title, just that he thought he'd found something big, and he had a lot of clients vying for it."

"And Victor was using Frederick's email to communicate with his customers about these first editions he was selling?" Willow asked.

Johnathan inclined his head. "That's what it sounds like to me. Why else would Victor lock Frederick out? Plus, Frederick was as honest as they come. There's no way his customers would even guess what he sold them wasn't for real."

As Willow and Johnathan talked, Lou couldn't help but wonder if Johnathan could've had something to do with the murder. The killer had cut the tags out of Frederick's suit, after all. Maybe it had been Johnathan, hoping to cover his tracks. But then why stand up and announce who he was to them, tonight? And what was his motive? Kimberly had mentioned the cops earlier, so Johnathan knew they were talking to a cop, but he hadn't balked or made excuses to leave.

Lou made a mental note to tell Easton about him. She ran her fingers along the edge of his card in her pocket.

Willow's phone buzzed with an incoming message. "East's here to pick us up." She stood, grabbing her bag. "Thanks for talking to us," she said to Johnathan.

"Yes, thank you," Lou added with an uneasy smile. After gaining even more proof that it had been the fake first editions that had gotten Frederick killed, she was legitimately worried for her safety. She was happy to be getting out of there and sticking close to Easton.

Weaving their way back through the dark hallways, Willow and Lou carefully slipped out through the middle changing room in the vintage clothing store. The guy behind the counter, who Lou now realized was more of a bouncer than a salesperson, nodded in their direction as they left.

Easton's car waited for them at the curb outside. It was warm inside the car, and Lou bundled into the back seat this time, letting Willow have the front.

"Find something good?" Easton asked, gesturing to Willow's bag.

"Yeah, we found Kimberly." Willow waggled her eyebrows.

Easton turned toward her in surprise, then moved to unbuckle his seat belt.

"Don't bother. She's long gone." Willow held a hand out to stop him. "We questioned her."

"And learned more of the truth about what happened to Frederick." Lou wet her lips. "You guys went through everything at Victor's apartment, right?"

Easton drove. "Yeah."

"Did you find a first edition of J. D. Salinger's *The Catcher in the Rye* there?" she asked.

Easton laughed. "There wasn't a book in that entire place."

"Which means Kimberly was right; Victor gave it to the loan shark to cover his debts." Lou tapped her fingers on her leg as she thought. "But then why did they still kill him?"

Easton clicked on his blinker. "We don't know that they did. The fingers? That was almost definitely them. There's a local loan shark who earned the nickname Tony Two Fingers because he always takes two fingers from the people who don't pay him on time. But Victor was hit by a semitruck. That could've just been terrible luck." Easton took a turn onto the road that would lead them out of Kirk.

Lou's phone flashed with a security notice. There was movement in the shop. Her heart pounded. When Willow mentioned they might be out late, Lou had put all the cats upstairs when she'd left earlier so they wouldn't trip the interior motion camera. That meant whatever motion was inside the bookshop was a person, possibly a killer.

It seemed as if every muscle in Lou's body tightened in anticipation as she clicked the button to go to the live feed in her shop. Her body relaxed as Lou watched a parade of cats spill into the bookshop, led by none other than little Romeow.

"Everything okay?" Willow asked, noticing Lou's frown as she checked her phone.

"Yeah," Lou said. "I got a movement notification from inside the shop, but I just have escaped cats instead of actual cat burglars. Though time will only tell what trouble Romeow will get up to with my new books." She groaned and set the snooze button on the cameras, knowing she didn't want to see all the damage when she had no way of getting back any sooner.

Willow groaned. "Oh no. Sorry. But the others are fine around the books, right? It's just him?"

"Just him." Lou puffed out her cheeks. "I feel bad. He's so sweet, but he just cannot live in a bookstore. Noah said he's trying to find someone to take him as quickly as possible."

Turning her attention away from the unavoidable disaster inside the bookshop, Lou focused on the case once more. "Okay, so Victor got into trouble with this Tony Two Fingers for not paying his debts on time," Lou recapped. "They beat him up and kidnapped him, cutting off a couple fingers."

"Kimberly mentioned his apartment was ransacked, and there were drops of blood on the floor," Willow reasoned, following along.

"Right," Lou said. "But if Victor sold some of the fake first editions and kept all the money to himself, wouldn't he have the money to pay off his debts? He didn't save any for Kimberly."

Easton clicked his tongue. "Depends on how much he was in for and what kind of vig they were charging him. The amounts these people deal in would surprise most folks."

"Vig?" Willow asked.

"It's an inflated interest rate," Easton explained.

Lou's eyebrows raised. "Okay, so what if he paid them, but it still wasn't enough? That's why he had to resort to telling them about his brother's valuable book."

"Maybe these guys went to Frederick to get it, but he ran, they chased him down and killed him in Lou's alley," Willow continued Lou's thought.

"Victor found the book for them, and once he was free, he was so relieved that he didn't pay attention to where he was walking and got hit by a semitruck?" Lou scratched at her cheek. Something about it didn't feel right.

In the rearview mirror, Easton's forehead creased as if he shared in her concern. "Tony might be awful, but he's not a killer. And Frederick doesn't sound like someone who would put a book before his life. I'm sure he would've handed it over if they'd threatened him. Tony doesn't do anything that might implicate him in court. We've been trying to nail him down for something ever since I first started on the force over a decade ago."

"What if the two brothers' deaths aren't connected, then?" Lou asked. "I mean, they are because it was Victor's actions that got Frederick killed, but what if a person angry about the fake first editions killed Frederick, and Victor died because he was relieved after paying off his debt with the copy of *The Catcher in the Rye*?"

"That could be." Easton nodded.

They worked through a few more scenarios as Easton drove toward Button. The case took Lou's mind off the mess Romeow was probably making in her bookstore. When Easton dropped Lou off, she waved good night, the fatigue of the day weighing heavily on her shoulders. All she wanted to do was head upstairs and go to sleep. But she had to corral the cats and clean up whatever mess Romeow had made first. Unlocking the door, she squinted as she entered, like someone preparing to be socked in the stomach.

The bookshop was clean, no signs of damage anywhere. Lou's heart sank. No signs of the cats were anywhere either. Had Romeow learned to open the back door as well? Racing to the back of the shop, she checked, but that door was closed. The one leading up to her apartment was open, however, which wasn't a surprise since she'd seen the cats come down and into the bookshop. The thought stopped her. How *had* the cats opened the door?

Her answer came in the form of voices upstairs.

"It's not up here," a man said, then paused. There wasn't a sound, and then he said, "Yeah, we checked downstairs too." He must've been on the phone.

Lou froze for just a moment, but the sound of large boots stomping down the staircase jolted her back into action. Scooting around the corner, Lou tucked herself behind a book-shelf, cramming her body as close to the wall as possible. In a well-lit shop, she would've been visible, but one of the burnt-out overhead lights hung directly above her. It was the first time she could genuinely thank Kimberly for anything in the past couple of weeks.

Tucked away where she was, she spotted Sapphy hiding on a bookshelf. He blinked his bright blue eyes at her, but his head whipped to one side as he felt the vibration of the men's boots on the bookshop hardwoods.

"He could've lied to us, you know," one man said to the other as they stopped in the center of the shop. "That guy was a mess, real desperate. You could see it in his eyes."

The other man snorted. "Everybody seems desperate when they're about to lose a finger. What'd the guy expect when he only brought sixty K of the hundred twenty he owed? What I wanna know is why'd he hide this thing in some random bookshop?"

"Said he stole it while his brother was out of town and knew the guy would check his apartment when he saw it was missing," the first guy explained.

"Yeah, but it's not here. The owner chick left the bar over half an hour ago. We've gotta get out of here before she comes back." Through the space above the books, she could just catch a glimpse of a man with short-cropped hair. He rubbed the back of his neck nervously.

How did they know she'd been at The Vault? Did they have someone following her? Kimberly's pained expression and her announcement that she owed the wrong people money seemed suspicious now that Lou thought about it. She closed her eyes. Kimberly must owe Tony money as well. She'd sold them out.

"Tony's gonna be mad. With Vic dead, and his brother getting himself killed before we could talk to him, this is the only way for him to recover the rest of the money."

Two Fingers Tony. These were Tony's men, Lou realized.

"I can't believe Vic got himself run over by a semi." The guy shivered. "Gross."

The other man let out a husky laugh. "Yeah, we probably should've given the guy a ride home, huh? Or a pill for his fingers, at least. He was too far gone from the pain when he stumbled by that truck stop."

Lou's mind wanted to think through the implications of what these men were saying, but fear kept her from forming any rational thoughts. She couldn't even move.

"Well, would'ya look at this." Footsteps stopped right next to Lou.

She held her breath and closed her eyes.

CHAPTER 23

Lou was sure they'd found her.

"Pretty eyes, huh?" the man said, close enough to Lou that she could almost feel the heat coming off him.

Lou's whole body stiffened in surprise as she thought about what he'd said. *But my eyes are closed.*

"Yeah, pretty. Whatever," the other intruder said, annoyance sharpening his words. "No more cats. We've gotta get out of here."

Lou peeked her eyes open to see them staring at Sapphy. Their backs to her.

It felt like it took hours for them to walk toward the back of the bookshop, but it was probably only seconds. Lou waited a few beats longer than she needed to before she exhaled fully. She slunk down the wall, pulling her knees close to her chest. With trembling fingers, she called Easton.

"Hey," he answered on the second ring, his voice croaky with fatigue. "Everything okay?"

"Tony's guys broke into the bookshop. They were here

when I got home. I hid until they left." Her words jumbled together as the pent-up adrenaline pushed them forward too fast.

"What? Are you okay?" Easton sounded wide awake now.

Lou's fingers shook as she pushed a stray hair out of her face. "Yeah, I think so." She took her first deep breath since they'd left. "They don't have *The Catcher in the Rye*, Easton. Apparently, Victor told them he'd hidden it in the bookshop. He died before he could bring it to them."

"So it's there with you?" Easton asked.

"No. They didn't find it." Lou wasn't sure if that made her feel better or worse. "So unless Kimberly has any hidden containers in the wall like Frederick, maybe Victor was lying."

"But it wasn't at Frederick's, and it wasn't at Victor's. So if he didn't give it to Tony ..." Easton cut out while he seemed to ponder that. "Okay, I'm coming over with a crew. We'll finger-print the place and check your camera footage to see if we can get these guys on breaking and entering. It'll be something at least."

Lou checked her security app. None of the cameras were online. She glanced over at the interior camera behind the register. It hung from the wall like it had been smashed with a baseball bat. Her heart sank.

"It'll have to be fingerprints. They took out all the cameras, but you can look into that when you get here." She hung up and went over to pet Sapphy. "Hi, buddy. I'm sorry that was scary." She folded him into her arms. "Shall we find the others?"

She placed Sapph in the office with all the downstairs litter boxes. It was like a reverse game of sardines, the hiding game she and Willow used to play as kids. Instead of all the cats hiding in one spot, she found them scattered throughout the bookshop. Whenever she found a cat, she put them in the office and shut the door to keep them together.

Ten minutes later, she'd found five of the cats—everyone except Romeow.

"Where'd you get to, you little stinker?" Lou scanned the tops of the bookshelves, his favorite hiding spot.

No orange kitten.

Fear clenched at her throat as she considered the possibility that he could've snuck out with the burglars. She ran back there to check. But even though the back lock was broken, the door was shut. She checked the alley behind the shop, then she ran upstairs.

No Romeow.

Lou sat on the floor of the bookshop and called him, hoping he'd come to her if she stayed in one spot long enough. She felt awful for how much she'd let herself get annoyed with the kitten. Now all she wanted was for him to be ripping up a book or hunting her from a bookshelf. As she sat there, her mind drifted to the case.

So Victor really had just died from a freak accident. He wasn't relieved, like she first thought. He was panicked. He probably hadn't been paying attention and had walked in front of the truck, too late. And they'd mentioned Frederick dying before they could talk to him. They hadn't been the ones to kill him, which meant it had to be someone angry about the fake first editions.

Lou took out her phone and consulted the picture she'd taken of the book page Noah had found on her table, the one Frederick had been clutching. It had been a list of names with titles next to them. She sucked in a breath as she saw *The Catcher in the Rye* had been one of the titles. It was next to the name Gerald.

She squinted as she thought. That name sounded familiar.

Lou gasped as she remembered. Johnathan had mentioned Gerald. He'd pointed at the bartenders at The Vault when he'd said it. He'd mentioned how he'd made Gerald's suits too. They hadn't worn name tags, but Lou knew which one was Gerald.

The man who'd stopped by the store the day after Frederick had been killed. Gerald had asked if she had any Bradbury or Salinger. Lou shivered, realizing that if Gerald and Frederick got custom suits from the same tailor, he would've known the tags inside would've led the police right to the tailor, and therefore to Frederick. He hadn't counted on Victor dying, leading the police to Frederick's identity. Without that happening, they might not have identified him for days or weeks more.

Gerald must've also known that Frederick had a copy of *The Catcher in the Rye*, so when he got that email from Victor acting as Freddie, he thought it was the real deal. Lou gasped. Gerald hadn't been looking for just any used Salinger that day. He'd been looking for the real first edition. The one he thought he'd bought from Frederick. How much had he paid for the fake? Had Victor gotten the full sixty thousand out of him Kimberly had mentioned it was worth? That would make someone mad enough to kill, for sure.

Lou almost clambered to her feet, but something under the bookshelf at the far end of the room caught her eye.

The swish of a thin orange tail.

"Romeow," Lou breathed out his name along with an exhale of relief. She crawled forward on her hands and knees until she was in front of the bookshelf.

Pressing her cheek to the floor, she peered into the space

under the bookshelf. It had to be just a few inches high. The kitten tilted its head to one side playfully and meowed at her.

"You really squeezed yourself in here, huh?" She chuckled. "It's safe to come out now." Lou contemplated grabbing a few pieces of cat food to lure him out, but before she could move, the kitten shot out from underneath the bookshelf and raced away.

She couldn't see where he'd gone.

Lou was about to stand up when she noticed there was still something underneath the bookshelf. It was a book. Sliding it out, Lou studied it. Her heartbeat sped up as she recognized it as a copy of J. D. Salinger's *The Catcher in the Rye*.

It couldn't be. Could it?

She flipped open the book. The copyright page held an authentic *first edition*, unlike the ones she'd found in the box in Frederick's safe. And on the title page, there was a signature from the author. But it wasn't just any signature. It held the author's childhood nickname, *Sonny Salinger*. This was the copy Kimberly had talked about.

She got to her feet and turned around, still gripping the book.

And then she froze. A man stood in her bookshop. He pointed a gun straight at her.

"I'll take that," he said, his words wobbling almost as much as his hands.

Gerald. Of course. He'd been at The Vault behind the bar tonight, and he'd come by the store after they'd found Frederick. Why hadn't she seen it before?

Lou's eyes flicked to the front door. She'd locked it behind her. Her heart sank as she remembered the back lock had been busted from the break-in. Gerald must've slipped inside

207

through the busted door while she was searching for the kitten.

He motioned to the book with his gun. "Just give it to me and no one has to get hurt. It's mine. I paid for it, fair and square. Give me the book and I'll leave."

Lou frowned as she realized he was right. If he'd paid Victor, he had paid for the fake version, thinking he was finally getting Frederick to part with his signed first edition. But his wording stuck out to Lou. *Give me the book and I'll leave.* He hadn't mentioned Frederick at all.

Why *would* Gerald suspect she knew he'd killed Frederick? She'd only just put it together herself. A lightness filled her. He was just here for the book, not to kill her.

All she had to do was hand him the book and he would leave. Then she could share her suspicions with Easton once he arrived, once they were safe.

Lou held the book forward warily. "It's yours."

Gerald's expression darkened like he thought it might be a trick. "You're going to give it up that easily, even after you stored it here for him all this time?"

Lou stepped closer. "I didn't know he'd stored it here," Lou said.

At this, Gerald scowled. "Of course you did. I saw him come here that Friday. I followed him here. He must've dropped it off with you. That's the only thing that makes sense." Gerald's hands shook even more.

"Please, just take it." With one last, careful step, Lou reached the book toward Gerald.

He took one of his hands off the handle of the gun. He snatched the book from her grasp, holding it tight to his body as if she might try to pry it back. Then he backed away, toward the broken door leading to the alley. Lou stood stock still, any relief on hold as she waited for him to leave her sight. He was almost gone. Just a few more feet and she'd be safe.

Before Gerald could take another step back, movement out the front window stole away his attention. Lou's eyes flicked over to see Easton's car and a police cruiser screech to a stop in front of the bookshop.

She'd been so close. This was one time she would've rather had the police stay away for just a few more minutes. Lou's stomach dropped as she turned back toward Frederick's killer.

CHAPTER 24

Gerald growled in frustration. "You called the cops? How?" He glanced behind him and then back to the front door as Easton tried the handle and realized it was locked.

Easton's eyes locked on to Gerald's gun and he yelled, "We're coming, Lou. Hang in there." One of the cops followed Detective West around to the alley while the other stayed to guard the front door and drew his gun.

Seeing his escape route was going to be blocked, Gerald stepped forward and grabbed her. Lou tried to elbow him, but he was too strong. He wrapped one arm around her, the book clutched tight between them, digging into her arm. With the other hand, he moved the gun so it pointed at her head.

The room spun around Lou as Easton and two uniformed officers slowly moved into the room, their guns drawn.

"Drop the weapon." Easton's eyes flicked up and down Lou to make sure she was okay.

"Just let me leave and I won't hurt her." Gerald's hand

shook, making the metal of the gun press into Lou's temple in an unsteady rhythm that only made her more nervous.

What if he accidentally pulled the trigger? She wanted to close her eyes.

He backed up, pulling her with him. "I paid for this book. I can show you the receipt. This is mine, fair and square." Taking another step, Gerald came to a stop as he backed into a bookshelf.

"Then why are you holding a gun to her head?" Easton asked—a good question Gerald hadn't seemed to consider.

Lou wet her lips, unsure what to do. "Easton, I think maybe we should just let him leave with the book," she said calmly.

But just as Easton was about to respond, his gaze flitted up above them at something. Movement must've caught his eye above their heads.

Movement toward the top of the bookshelf.

Immediately, Lou knew what was about to happen. She tried not to tense but steadied her breathing in the split second she had before—

"ARGH!" Gerald screamed as Romeow's claws sank into his scalp.

Lou ducked out from under Gerald's arm as he moved to pry the cat off his head. The book dropped, and his gun clattered to the floor. When Lou looked up, Romeow was flying through the air, eyes wide and claws extended. Gerald must've thrown him off. Lou caught the kitten and ducked to hide between the bookshelves.

Whereas she'd run *away* from Gerald, Easton ran *toward* him. The man let out an *oomph* as Easton tackled him to the ground, reading him his rights as he pulled his arms behind his back to be handcuffed.

"You're under arrest for armed robbery and assault." Easton clicked the handcuffs into place and then stood, pulling Gerald to his feet as well.

"And for the murder of Frederick Alvarado," Lou said, peeking around the bookshelf she'd hidden behind with Romeow.

Easton's eyes went wide, and then understanding fell over his features.

Gerald watched her in stunned silence.

"Though, I'm thinking that might've been an accident," Lou said, studying the man who'd just held her at gunpoint. She walked forward and plucked the copy of *The Catcher in the Rye* off the floor and held it out toward one of the other officers since Easton had his hands full.

"He fell. It was an accident." The words tore out of Gerald. They seemed to rip him in half to admit out loud. "I mean, I pushed him, but he tripped and fell back and hit his head." Tears streamed down Gerald's face. "I was so angry. I was so sure he'd tried to pull one over on me."

"But it was Victor the whole time." Lou pressed her lips together, knowing this would probably come as a shock to Gerald. He'd been too far away from their table tonight to hear the truth from Kimberly. "Victor used Frederick's email to contact you about the book. I'm guessing he mailed it to you instead of dropping it off in person?"

Gerald's expression fell. "But I thought—" His voice split. "That had been more proof that he'd been trying to pull one over on me." The man's shoulders sank forward.

Lou's heart broke. He was a desperate, crazed man, but he hadn't planned on killing Frederick.

"Okay, let's get you out of here," Easton said, pushing him forward. He unlocked the front door of the bookshop and put

Gerald into the back of the police cruiser. The uniformed officers drove off with the criminal, but Easton came back inside.

"How did you know?" he asked, running a hand through his hair.

Lou set Romeow down on the floor since he'd started to squirm. "I figured it out just before you got here. I was going to tell you my theory, but Gerald showed up first." She explained how she'd remembered the names on the book page Frederick had left behind. She put that together with Johnathan saying he'd made suits for Gerald at the bar, so he would've known about cutting the tags. She even explained how he'd stopped by to look for the book the day after he'd killed Frederick, sure she was hiding it for him.

Easton shook his head. "You're right, without Victor's death, we might not have found out Frederick's identity as quickly." He looked around. "Okay, I'm going to fingerprint the place, see if we can't get something on Tony's guys."

"Thanks," she said. But just as she was about to sit down, another car pulled up—screeched to a halt—in front of the shop was actually more like it. Willow's car.

Lou turned toward Easton, who said, "I texted her. Thought you might need a friend after all of that."

Relief settled over Lou as her best friend barreled into the shop and pulled her into a too-tight hug.

"Honest three." Willow's voice shook.

"Scared, relieved, sad." The last word came out small. Lou couldn't help but feel bad for Frederick, for all of them, actually.

They'd all gotten caught up in this because of greed—whether it was Gerald's need to own that first edition or Victor's misuse of money. In the end, poor Frederick had paid the ultimate price.

CHAPTER 25

L ou stood outside of the bookstore and surveyed the artist as he finished the last few strokes. In each of the two front windows, the new shop name was printed in a beautiful thin serif font.

Whiskers and Words.

A huge smile peeled over Lou's face. It was perfect. The Japanese magnolia trees had held on to their white blossoms, but only barely. That was okay. Lou had only hoped they would last until her grand reopening tonight. And now, that was just a few hours away.

She admired the newly painted sign that hung over the front door, too, with the bookshop's new name. Everything was coming together. She thanked the artist as they cleaned up and headed inside.

The bookstore looked amazing.

All the overhead lights were now working, thanks to Noah and his tall ladder. They complemented the antique lamps Lou had purchased from Smitty at the antique store, giving a balanced feel of cozy warmth and good lighting. Speaking of cozy, Lou appraised the new furniture set that Bea had delivered from The Upholstered Button. It was gorgeous, especially accented with the soft throws Lou had draped on each seat. The tweedy gray fabric of the couch and matching chairs were so inviting, Lou would've curled up on the love seat if she hadn't had a million things to do.

"What about this area here?" Willow asked Lou. She stood over by the cash register and held the cat adoption profiles up, her fingers holding pieces of tape. Along with the cat profile sheets, Lou had printed out the T. S. Eliot poem about the naming of cats, to hang alongside.

"That looks great, though I'll have to move them to a place with more room if I get many more." Lou cringed. Right now, the idea of even one more cat seemed like a lot.

But she was growing to love them all. She'd had too much fun documenting their likes and dislikes for their humorous adoption profile sheets. Willow chuckled as she hung each one and read over them.

"I don't even want a cat, and this makes me want to take at least one of them home." Willow glanced over her shoulder.

"That's the hope," Lou said. "Maybe we should print a second set for the window too?" Lou suggested. Willow gave her a thumbs-up and went to take care of it.

The cupcakes were already set up on the table, but they were covered so no cats could get into them. Next to them, carafes holding coffee and hot water sat at the ready. New and used books stocked the shelves; bookish trinkets sat near the register, and best of all, the place felt alive once more.

Lou found Sapphire on a bookshelf, taking a nap. She

leaned forward and planted a kiss on his nose after tapping on the shelf to let him know she was there.

"We did it, Sapph," she whispered. "We made it even better." Stepping back, she beamed. "Ben would've loved it."

The white cat stretched out a paw, extended his claws, and then he went back to sleep. Lou took that to mean he agreed.

The bell on the front door chimed, and Lou peered over with worry. The reopening didn't start for two hours. She still had to brush all the cats and put Sapphire's new collar on. She'd gotten a special collar printed with the words **Not for adoption,** so people wouldn't get confused and try to take him home.

But any worry Lou felt drifted away as she turned to see Noah walk inside, Marigold at his heels. Those two had been such a help in the last few days, they were welcome anytime. Lou felt that statement even more as she saw what they carried with them. They each held three cozy fleece cat beds.

"We made these for the cats," Marigold said as she held one forward for Lou to inspect.

The fleece was so soft Lou wanted to brush it against her cheek. The fabric of each bed had a unique pattern of cat paws or books. They didn't have sides, but were more of a small, padded rectangle, which meant they would fit on the bookshelves too.

"I love them." Lou hugged the one she held to her. "Thank you so much," she said, looking first to Marigold and then Noah.

"Dad did most of the sewing," Marigold whispered, leaning forward. "I mostly just stuffed them with the fluff."

Lou chuckled. "That's an important job." She glanced over at the cats congregating around them, trying to smell the beds as if they already knew they were for them. "Speaking of important jobs," Lou said to Marigold as she picked up a small brush, "I have one you can help me with."

Lou's heart soared as she saw the lineup of customers and locals who'd shown up for the reopening. Everyone loved the new name and thought the sign looked wonderful.

Noah and Marigold had stuck around. Marigold brushed all the cats for Lou, which turned out to be perfect since she got called aside to do a quick interview for the *Button Post*. Easton stopped by to say hello and grab a copy of *The Catcher in the Rye*—just a regular one, not the signed first edition.

"Gotta see what all the fuss was about," he said with a smirk as he paid her for the book and left.

He'd been able to get fingerprints off the doors from that night. Paired with the footage from the cameras before they'd been destroyed, it had been enough to arrest at least two of Tony's thugs for breaking and entering and send Tony a much-deserved warning.

About an hour into the reopening, George stepped up to the counter with a new *Star Wars* novel clutched in her hands. She'd helped Lou with a new set of cameras.

During hour two of the three-hour opening event, a young woman walked tentatively through the front door. She glanced around warily as if she expected someone to come tell her to leave at any moment.

Lou walked over to her, wearing a big smile. "Welcome to Whiskers and Words. Is there a book I can help you find?"

The woman rubbed at her elbow. "To be honest, I don't really like books. I can't tell you the last time I bought a book, let alone read one." She snorted out a laugh. "I mostly came in because I saw the pictures of the cats," she said, gesturing back toward the front window where Willow had hung up a second set of the cat adoption profiles.

Lou's smile increased. "You're interested in adopting?"

The young woman dipped her head from one side to the next. "I've been looking for a cat. I thought it might be nice to come here and spend time with one to see how they are. I've never been able to get up the courage to go to one of those shelters where they're all in cages. It makes me too sad, and I end up wanting to take all of them home, which makes me feel awful because I know I can't."

"I know the feeling," Lou said, realizing she'd only ever imagined having one or two foster cats in the shop at a time, and she already had five her first week of business.

"Anything special you're searching for?" Lou asked, directing the woman to the adoption posters inside.

She shrugged. "Not really. I just thought I'd know if the right one was here. You know?"

Lou kept herself calm on the outside. Inside, she was ecstatic. This sounded too good to be true.

"So you really don't like books?" Lou asked, hoping the question didn't sound judgmental. She really just wanted to make sure.

The customer shook her head.

"How do you feel about sneak attacks?" Lou asked.

The young woman laughed. "Okay, I think."

"I might just I have the perfect guy for you, but why don't you spend some time with him first." Lou pointed out Romeow on the poster. "Let's go find the little heartbreaker."

They located the kitten hiding behind a bookshelf, just about to pounce on a little boy. Lou gave the customer a *See? I told you so* look as she picked him up and handed him over.

"He hates books too," Lou told her as she cuddled the kitten. "Rips them up into shreds anytime he can get his claws on one."

The happiness evident on that customer's face as she held the orange kitten made it all worth it for Lou.

"There are couches and chairs if you want to sit." Lou motioned to the furniture she'd just purchased. "Feel free to make yourself comfortable while you get to know him."

It was a good thing Noah stuck around for the opening because the woman, who turned out to be named Kayla, adopted Romeow. Noah handled the paperwork, since Lou had her hands full with more customers.

The whole town of Button seemed to show up. Cassidy came by with a bottle of champagne for Lou to celebrate. Not only did all the owners of the shops she'd visited stop by—Bea, Smitty, and Lindsey—but Lou even caught a glimpse of the bowler-hat guy she'd talked to her first time in the coffee shop. He had a book in one hand and a cat curled in his lap as he sat in one of the new chairs.

All in all, it was a roaring success. Three hours had been perfect, Lou realized, because she was beat by the time the last customer left. Then it was just Lou and Willow.

The two friends locked the front door to the bookshop and then wrapped an arm around each other, leaning their heads together—as much as that worked with their height difference.

"Ben would love it," Willow said as they gazed around the bookshop.

Lou sighed. "He does," she said with all the confidence in the world. She could feel it.

WHISKERS AND WORDS WILL RETURN ...

Pick up the second book in the series.

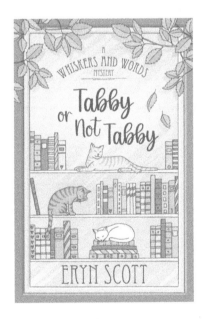

For a town that's as cute as a button, there sure is a lot of murder.

Louisa Henry's dream bookshop is up and running. On a trip to deliver a book to one of her customers, Lou stumbles upon the man's dead body. The police are sure it's a suicide, but Lou has questions. Clues at the scene, as well as details about the man's life, just don't seem to add up.

The fact that the dead man was the town bully is only one of many things that gives Lou pause. Are the police jumping to the conclusion of suicide so they don't have to arrest the person who did everyone a favor?

Lou's also busy helping her best friend, Willow, with preparations for the high school's annual Spring Fling. But during her time at the drafty old building, Lou finds secrets hidden away no one was meant to see, and she learns her new town might be hiding more than she first thought.

Buy Today!

Join Eryn Scott's mailing list to learn about new releases and sales!

ALSO BY ERYN SCOTT

MYSTERY:

The Pepper Brooks Cozy Mystery Series

Pebble Cove Teahouse Mysteries

The Stoneybrook Mysteries

Whiskers and Words Mysteries

WOMEN'S FICTION:

The Beauty of Perhaps

Settling Up

The What's in a Name Series

In Her Way

I Pick You

ROMANTIC COMEDY:

Meet Me in the Middle

About the Author

Eryn Scott lives in the Pacific Northwest with her husband and their quirky animals. She loves classic literature, musicals, knitting, and hiking. She writes cozy mysteries and women's fiction.

Join her mailing list to learn about new releases and sales!

www.erynscott.com

Lightning Source UK Ltd.
Milton Keynes UK
UKHW011807260722
406402UK00002B/707